Love Came Down At Christmas

A *Fancy* Amish Smicksburg Tale

Karen Anna Vogel

Lamb Books

Love Came Down At Christmas: A Fancy Amish Smicksburg Tale

© 2014 by Karen Anna Vogel

ISBN-13: 978-0692349557
ISBN-10: 0692349553
Lamb Books

This book is a work of fiction. The names, characters, places, and incidents are products of the writer's imagination or have been used fictitiously and are not to be construed as real. Any resemblance to persons, living or dead, actual events, locales or organizations is entirely coincidental.

Contact the author on Facebook at:
www.facebook.com/VogelReaders

Learn more the author at: www.karenannavogel.com

Visit her blog, Amish Crossings, at
www.karenannavogel.blogspot.com

*Dedicated to
young and old who feel alone on
Christmas. You are loved.*

*I have loved you with an everlasting love; I have drawn
you with unfailing kindness....*

Jeremiah 31:3 NIV

*Look! I stand at the door and knock. If you hear my
voice and open the door, I will come in, and we will share
a meal together as friends.*

Revelation 3:20 NLT

We love because God first loved us.

1 John 4:19 ISV

.

Table of Contents

Amish – English Dictionary

Pennsylvania Dutch dialect is used throughout this book, common to the Amish of Western Pennsylvania. You may want to refer to this little dictionary from time to time.

Ach – oh

Danki – thank you

Dawdyhaus – grandparent's house

Furhoodled –Mixed up in the head, confused.

Gut – good

Jah - yes

Kinner – children

Nee- no

Mamm – mom

Oma – grandma

Opa –grandfather

Wunderbar – wonderful

Yinz – Western Pennsylvania slang for "you ones" or "you all"

.

Chapter 1

Change, Change, Change!

Lexi Remington stared in disbelief at her foster mother. *Tricia was going back to her parents?* Tricia, who was in the same sixth grade class as her, who she told all her secrets to, would be leaving Smicksburg to live in Pittsburgh? Sixty miles away? *Change, change, change*, she wanted to scream. "Life stinks" was all Lexi could get out, her heart stuck in her throat.

Angela Stotler grabbed Lexi's hand across the kitchen table. "I understand."

Anger arose in Lexi. Angela had a perfect life. A nice house in Amish country, *family*, all Lexi wanted. No, Angela did not understand. But she'd come to love Angela over the past two years, feeling closer to her than her natural parents. But then who wouldn't, since her real parents were in jail.

"Want to help me decorate for Thanksgiving this week? Ali and Elyse will be home from college tomorrow. Excited about that?" Angela asked, forcing a smile.

Lexi looked around the cozy kitchen. It was almost all windows, shelves lined to place plates, cups, canisters and all the many baskets Angela bought from Amish friends. Lexi felt more at home in this kitchen than anywhere else in this cozy little Cape Cod house. But with Ali and Elyse coming home, emptiness enveloped her soul. They were Angela's real kids and jealousy always choked Lexi when they came home.

Angela placed a newspaper on the table. "Look over the Black Friday sales. Want to go out again at the crack of dawn like last year?"

"Will Tricia be going?"

Angela's tall slender body slowly arose and leaned over her open dishwasher, rearranging the plates. "No, just you and me this year. She'll be back with her folks for Thanksgiving."

Lexi saw Angela bite her lower lip as her chin started to quiver. She turned towards the sink full of dishes but her shoulders were shaking. Tricia had lived with the Stotlers for a whole year and her foster mom's heart was broken. Lexi ran to her and hugged her from behind. "I'm still here." Angela grabbed a tissue out of her jean pocket and dabbed her eyes, and then spun around and kissed the top of Lexi's head. "I'm sorry. Of course, I still have you and we'll have the best holiday season ever."

A flicker of warmth lit Lexi's heart. "I wish Tricia could shop with us again."

"Well, Judy thought a holiday would make for a good reunion," Angela said, as tears glistened in her mellow blue eyes. "Judy said I have some homework to do…"

"Ugh. Homework," Lexi growled.

Angela forced a grin. "I know how much you love yours."

"More paperwork for being a foster mom? More classes?" Lexi held her breath, fearing Angela's big heart would want another child soon, and no one could take Tricia's place. No one. And she sure didn't want a foster brother. Boys were mean in school. Men were mean, all of them, just like her dad.

"Judy said my homework is to…work on not getting so attached to my foster kids but I can't help it. Maybe I'm not cut out for it."

"What?" Lexi blurted. "Get rid of me?"

"No, no. You're my girl and can stay here." She picked up one of her many tea pots from a shelf. "Want some peppermint tea?"

Lexi could stand it no more. She'd been trying to learn manners, hold her tongue but Angela was too hard on herself. "Judy's wrong. You make us feel loved. What's wrong with that?"

Angela's blonde hair fell over her shoulders as she filled the tea pot with water. "Judy is a wonderful woman, a social worker with a tender heart. She gives me advice. The goal of a foster parent is to help reunite kids with their parents, if possible. But…"

"What?"

"I pray you're with us for" – Angela stopped abruptly.

"Lexi, you know how John and I feel about you…"

A mixture of comfort and fear ran through Lexi. Why was Angela acting do odd? Would she be leaving, too?" *Best not ask.* Angela wasn't told much anyhow. All she and John, her husband, could do was stand-in. Stand in place of her parents until they were either rehabilitated or deemed unfit and then Lexi could be adopted by *real* parents.

Angela put the tea pot on the stove and then met Lexi's gaze, her eyes misted. "Regrets over yesterday and the fear of tomorrow are twin thieves that rob us of the moment. Emma always says that and it's true. We can't change the past and worry does us no good."

Lexi caught Angela's meaning. Forgive and move forward, like her Amish neighbor Emma always said. Living among the Amish in Smicksburg was a blessing and a curse. A blessing because Amish girls her age were more mature and thought of more things than boys, and Lexi was learning so much about farm animals, but it was also a curse because Amish families were huge, some having ten kids or more, and it only made her know what she would never have…a family.

~*~

Emma pulled the final stitch through the baby quilt, knotted the thread and then snapped it off. She held the blanket out and a sense of satisfaction ran through her veins. "*Ach*, it's beautiful," she chimed.

The knock on her front door told Emma an *Englisher* had arrived. All Amish knew to use the side door right into the kitchen where baked goods and warm coffee could be had along with good conversation. Placing the quilt on a side table, she crossed the tiny living room to see who was visiting. Through the top glass panels she saw Lexi...and she was crying. Welcoming the dear girl and cold winter air into the living room of her tiny dawdyhaus, she asked the Lord above to give her words again to say. "Lexi, what's ailing you?"

Lexi flung her arms around Emma who was only a tad bit taller than her. "Tricia, she's leaving. Going back to..."

"Her real parents?"

Lexi sobbed uncontrollably but was able to get out, "Angela's like a *real* mom."

Emma pat her back. "And John, too?"

Lexi shrugged.

Emma took a package of Kleenex out of her apron. "Here. Now you go ahead and let those tears flow. I've never seen them."

"What?"

"Your tears. It's *gut* to cry. Cleans out the body."

"But it makes me feel sick. I've been so tired."

Emma's soft gray eyes misted. "It's part of being a feeling person. You care a lot in here." She pointed to Lexi's heart. "You've changed since you came."

"How?" Lexi asked, untying the laces from her boots.

"You showed so little emotion when I first met you, only anger. But I could see it was hurt. Now, here you are able to love. It's a miracle."

Lexi stood up and jutted out her chin. "You thought it was impossible for me to love someone?"

"*Nee*, not at all. What I mean is a *gut* change." Emma went over to her rocker and lifted up the new baby quilt. "What do you think?"

"Will someone buy it or is it an order?" Lexi asked.

"It's to go in the quilt shop. I sure hope it fetches a *gut* price."

Lexi took off her red winter coat and hung it on a peg near the door and then crossed the room to sit in a rocker near Emma. "Are you still worried?"

"Not worried, just…concerned." Emma grabbed a stuffed calico heart hung by a ribbon. "Do you think the English will hang these on their trees?"

"I would. Angela would. She loves homemade ornaments."

"Then this is what we'll work on. We'll hang them on the window of the shop like they do in town. Such a *gut* idea to have things in windows so customers can see from the road."

Lexi offered a faint smile. "Angela said when she was little, she'd go window shopping."

Emma stared at the Christmas heart ornament. "Atley used

to do that…"

"He would?"

Emma's countenance fell as she remembered how Atley went to three big stores to get the triple paned glass windows to keep their *dawdyhaus* snug in winter. "He loved to work with his hands…"

Lexi cocked her head. "Who did?"

"Atley. He designed this house, windows and all."

"I'm not talking about buying windows, but to look through them at displays. You know, how we're going to do with Christmas ornaments."

Emma covered her mouth in shame, and then smirked. "I thought of Atley immediately. Miss him horribly."

Lexi leaned back and glared at the ceiling. "Why can't life stay the same?"

"Get used to change my dear." Emma took Lexi's hand. "Life is full of it. I knew in my head my husband of fifty years would be taken someday, but never in my heart." She straightened and reached for a bolt of red material in her bin. "But we move forward, *jah*?"

Lexi squeezed Emma's hand. "I love it here with you. I never had a grandma. I'm really afraid."

Emma cocked her head back. *So much emotion and words strung together.* "Lexi, what are you afraid of?"

"My parents coming to get me. I'd run away if I had to go

back."

"Oh, precious one. Tricia having to leave makes you feel this way. But remember, until your parents are considered fit to be parents, you'll be with Angela and John."

"I love Angela."

"*And John?*"

"He's a man."

"Atley was a man…"

Lexi's brows furrowed and she was quiet for a spell. "He was old though."

"So?"

"He couldn't hurt me."

Emma passed the red material to Lexi. "Few men are like your *daed*. Alcohol made his temper worse, *jah?*"

"Yes." Lexi's nose twisted in disdain.

Emma leaned towards Lexi. "You know what? I'm determined that you and I are going to have a *wunderbar gut* Christmas despite our tears."

"Your tears? You cry, too?"

"*Jah*. No Atley this year. But I'll bake Christmas cookies, decorate the store and celebrate the true meaning and it'll lift me right up, and you, too."

Lexi got up and hugged Emma. "I love you."

Emma had never heard this from Lexi and warmth filled her heart for she'd come to deeply care for this little one like she were her own *grandkinner*. "And I love you."

~*~

Angela grabbed John's hand that night as they sat in the living room, Tricia and Lexi asleep upstairs. She caressed John's large masculine hand with her thumb. "I dread this…"

"We knew it was coming," John said, lips set in a grim line. "But Tricia's parents have obviously gotten better…"

"I hope so. It rips my heart out how parents can be so irresponsible."

"Look at what forgiveness has done to your parents. They're wonderful now."

"Well, I still have scars," Angela said, her forehead puckered. She was fifty, and chided herself for the vivid memories of her childhood, being slapped around by her father. She tried to count her blessings, saying she couldn't identify with foster children if she'd had a perfect childhood, but it still stung at times. The day her dad apologized and started to attend Alcoholics Anonymous was etched in her mind.

"Honey, what are you thinking?"

"Well, I'm nervous about Lexi, too. Only a month to go…"

"I know. I'm nervous, too." He opened their *Bible in a Year* book and flipped to the reading.

Angela leaned her head on his shoulder. "I love these quiet times we started. We stayed on track all year."

"Yep, we're at November twenty-four. Never thought we'd do it." He laid the book down on his lap. "Hey, Thanksgiving's late this year. Christmas is only a month away. Do we have enough money for gifts?"

"Well, we never splurge, you know. We get party favors. It's not our birthday." Angela looked up and pinched John's cheek. "Hey, Dimples, what do you want for Christmas?"

"Dimples? You haven't called me that in years. Think I have a baby-face or something?"

Angela ran her slender fingers over John's brown stubble. "Growing a beard for winter?"

"Why, do you want me to?"

"N-O," she spelled out. "I love to see your dimples, but if you stuff yourself over the holidays, they'll disappear."

He grabbed Angela around the waist, threatening her with a good tickle. "I put on fifteen pounds last year but took it off."

Angela squelched a scream and broke loose. "Stop it," she ran to the other side of the room and put a finger to her mouth. "If you tickle, I'll scream."

He put both hands up as if under arrest. "Okay, back to my question then. Have enough money for gifts?" John raked his fingers through his hair. "I don't want anything except…"

Angela's eyes met his, and yes, she knew. This Christmas was different. "All we can do is pray about it…"

Chapter 2

Second-Hand Nativity Set

Lexi hoped the hug Tricia gave her yesterday would not be the last. The room the girls shared now had only one bed and one dresser. She flung herself down on her single bed and started to daydream of Tricia and her being reunited. Tricia was her defender against the bullies and she just gave one a slug that left Jaden Anderson with a black eye. Then when Billy Blackwood pulled at her hair, there was Tricia, slamming him. Tricia was the tallest girl in the sixth grade. A bitter lump formed in Lexi's throat. She'd probably never see her friend again.

Maybe Angela could get her phone number and we could text? But then Lexi knew about rules! *So many rules in foster care!*

A wrap on the door with a familiar rhythm told her it was Ali. "Come in."

Ali peeked in. "Hey, kiddo. Why are you hiding in here? Come on. I bet I can beat you at checkers…as usual."

Wanting to crawl into a ball under her quilt, she shook her head.

11

"Oh, come on. I'm only home for a few days." Ali hooked two fingers on each end of her mouth to make a fake pout.

Ali had never made such an effort to spend time with her. *Was something wrong?* Would this be her last Thanksgiving with the Stotlers? Her heart tightened and the room began to swirl. "I'm not feeling good."

Ali, clad in a checkered flannel shirt with jeans tucked into leather boots sat down on the edge of the bed. Lexi looked into her light blue eyes. *Ali could be a model for a country magazine,* she thought. *Blue eyed and blonde like Angela.*

"Let me feel your forehead. Maybe a fever." Ali placed a frigidly cold hand on her forehead. "Nope, no fever."

"Your hands are ice."

"Hey, kiddo, I'm studying to be a nurse and I say you're not sick." Ali's face screwed up. "Just tired?"

"Suppose so."

"It's normal to feel depressed that Tricia's gone," Ali said softly, shoulders slouching. "I didn't know her as well as you, but she was a nice little girl. Hope things work out."

Lexi rolled her eyes. "Little girl? She's in the sixth grade."

Ali leaned over Lexi, her long hair cascading onto the bed. "Excuse me Ms. Lexi. I forgot. You're all grown up." She sprang up, put a finger to her chin and grinned. "And I know that grown-ups love to read."

"I don't," Lexi mumbled.

"You just need more practice." Ali snapped her fingers. "You love horses, right?"

"Ya, but –

"*Black Beauty*. You can borrow my copy, but be careful with it. Genuine Leather-bound."

Before any objection could be made, Ali darted out of the room. Lexi crawled under her covers, determined to have a good cry, taking Emma's advice. But soon her throat tightened. Why was Ali being so friendly? Ali never let her borrow anything. Shame slapped her in the face. *Because you used to steal, Lexi Remington*, she remembered. But Lexi did think it was odd how cozy Ali had suddenly become. Ali knew something, a secret, and it had to do with her. What was it?

~*~

John rubbed his sweaty palms on his jeans and then knocked on Lexi's door. "Can I come in?"

A ruffling of papers was heard, but no one spoke.

"Lexi, I'm leaving in half an hour to go to church. Remember? You promised you'd go to Wednesday night services."

Creaking boards and then a thud.

John froze. "Are you alright?"

"Tripped. Was coming to open the door." The brass doorknob turned and soon Lexi was looking at John wryly. "I changed my mind."

"Why?" John asked, but knew the answer.

"Angela's not going. It would be…"

"Just us?"

Lexi twirled a strand of brown hair around her finger. "Angela wants time with her real kids, huh? Wants me out of the house?"

John couldn't believe how fast Lexi could feel rejected. "Actually, Elyse's coming, too. She wants to see everyone."

Lexi reddened. "Well. Okay. But why isn't Angela coming?"

John crossed his arms. "You don't like me?"

"What?"

"You only want to spend time with Angela." He put a hand over his heart. "Am I right?"

Perspiration formed over her lips. "I, ah, get along better with…girls."

John planted his hands on her shoulders, eyeing her evenly. "Honey, I'm not your dad."

Lexi backed away, her face contorted. "I know that. I'm not stupid."

"What I mean is that your dad wasn't very nice to you. You think all men are mean now."

Lexi's eyes brimmed with tears. "It's true," she blurted.

John stepped back, shocked by the force of Lexi's emotions. She was always stone-faced, never crying. Here she was, appearing vulnerable. How could he help her? *One plank at a time,* he thought, remembering a Sunday school lesson. "Lexi, when you build a bridge, you use planks, right?"

Her brow furrowed. "No. You use steel or some other metal."

"Okay, pretend it's a jungle type bridge made of wooden planks. You'd need planks." He scratched his chin. "You need to build a bridge of trust. There has to be one man in all your twelve years that you thought was nice. One you trusted."

Lexi grabbed the doorknob to shut him out, but John put his hand on hers. "I know it's painful, but think."

She pulled away, clenching her fists and jabbed them on her sides. "How do you know it's hard?"

John stuffed his hands into his jean pockets. She was right. He didn't know. But then he thought of Max. "I got bit by a huge dog when I was a kid. After that, I was afraid of a toy poodle. I saw all dogs as mean." He straightened. "So, my grandpa made me walk the next door neighbors dog so I'd overcome my fears. It worked. I trusted one dog and then another and I, well, overcame my fear of dogs."

Lexi looked unflinching at John. "Mr. Beech."

"What?"

"Mr. Beech. He was my neighbor and he tried to help. I'd run to his house and he gave me food."

John gulped. "Were you hungry?"

"Only beer in the fridge. Mr. Beech bought groceries just for me. He was old and his niece took him shopping. She showed me the list and asked if there was anything else I needed."

John leaned on the door frame. "Plank one. Mr. Beech was like a guardian angel."

Lexi stared at the floor. "And Atley."

"Atley was a good man," John said. "Matthew running off put him in an early grave."

"What?" Lexi barked.

"Emma's grandson ran off and broke Atley's heart." John rubbed a hand over his dark stubble. "Why are you mad?"

Lexi slammed the door in record time. *Must have hit a nerve*, John thought. "Lexi, no slamming doors."

"Alright!" she yelled.

"Be ready in fifteen minutes."

"Alright again," she hissed.

~*~

That night at church, Pastor Dale wore a bright red tie dotted with small green Christmas trees. *How nerdy*, Lexi thought. Then her mind drifted to Black Friday shopping with Angela. She'd get a tie like that for John. He was a nerd. *And too pushy. And judgmental.* Her dad always said *Lexi, you'll put me in an early grave. If only she could…*

Elyse got up and started to address the packed out

congregation. This was not a boring Wednesday night Bible study, Lexi thought. It was Light-Up-Night planning meeting. *Why did John insist she come?*

Elyse, who was a year older than Ali and in her last year of college, had dark features like John. She flipped her shoulder-length brown hair behind her pink sweater. "Pastor Dale found a great deal on Craigslist: a life-sized nativity set. But it needs lots of work. Cleaned, repainted, and Joseph's hands are missing. One of the Three Wise men has also lost his crown," she beamed, "and we must treat royalty a little better. How about we restore the whole set and put it in front of the tree?"

Whispers echoed throughout the church and then, Gus, the elderly church janitor raised his hand. "Count me in." Others followed but to Lexi's irritation, John said he'd give Joseph new hands. *He was a carpenter after-all and needed them.* Lexi rolled her eyes. *How corny.*

Elyse laughed. "Good one, Dad." She shifted and her eyes landed on her boyfriend, Mike, who stared at her with puppy dog eyes. "I won't be home until a week before Christmas, not able to supervise it all, but I thought *yinz* could all meet here at the church and work together…over hot chocolate."

"Good idea," said Debbie, Pastor Dale's wife. "We all need more bonding time at Christmas and we can all focus on its real meaning."

"If it keeps my wife out of the stores, let's do it," Charles, the church pianist shouted with a whoop. His wife nudged him and he let out an "Oops."

"How about the bake sale?" Mary Lou, the one who made pastries for The Sampler asked. "It's not Christmas without lots of cookies."

Dale mounted the platform, patting Elyse on the back and turned to his congregation. "We can do that, too, Ester. We're all open to suggestions."

Lexi thought of the stuffed heart ornaments. Emma needed money to keep her quilt shop open. She waved to Elyse as their eyes met before she sat down next to Mike. Elyse squinted and pointed to Lexi. "I think Lexi has an idea. What is it honey?

Lexi wanted to be one with the wooden church pew, sink into it and never reappear. *Honey? When would she be treated like an adult?*

"Go on," Pastor Dale urged.

"Ah, how about we sell some Amish crafts?"

"The town is flooded with tourists on Light-Up Night," Elyse said. We could advertise for the Amish by giving out maps to all their stores."

A loud silence echo across the church. A huff was heard and then someone spoke up. It was Nelda, the church gossip and divider. "We pay higher taxes because of them. I say no. Let them fend for themselves."

John stood up. "They pay all the taxes we do plus never ask us for a dime for their schoolhouses."

"They don't have to pay social security," Nelda challenged.

"They opted out as a community long ago. They take care of their elderly. They don't want any government handouts."

"And maybe that's why they need more money." Nelda stood her ground.

Lexi felt her eyes near bulge out of her head with fury. She shot up and met Nelda's grim eyes. "Do you know how hard they work?"

"Hard times have fallen on us all. Emma Yoder's quilt shop may close," John said, defending Lexi.

"Oh, I love her store," Debbie whined. "How about if we only include stores that are hurting. Some aren't as they're on major roads. What do *yinz* say?"

Heads began to nod and Lexi looked up at John. He stood up for her. Why? But then she knew how close the Stotlers were with the big Yoder clan next door.

John looked down with pride as the congregation agreed to her idea. He leaned over and whispered, "Someone has to stand up to that big old bully."

Nervous laughter burst forth from Lexi. "Ya, she's old."

He put an arm around her. "I meant the bully part. Nelda's my age."

Lexi pulled away out of habit and instantly John's

shoulders slumped and his eyes looked tired. Why?

Chapter 3

Thanksgiving Dinner Dysfunction

*A*ngela closed the desk drawer in the living room and locked it.

"Why the lock?" Ali asked.

Angela fumbled for words, and then said, "I'm going shopping tomorrow, remember. Up at four like the Amish."

"Black Friday! Yay!" Ali screamed. "How could I forget?"

"Finals, that's how," Angela reminded her.

Ali moaned. "I can't go. I have gobs of studying to do. Classes start back up Monday."

Angela heard the timer go off and ran to the stove. She yelled over to the living room. "We all have to make sacrifices, Ali. I haven't seen the Macy's Day Parade in twenty years."

"Aw, Mom," Elyse said, taking the baster out of Angela's hand. "Go watch it. I'll take care of the turkey."

Angela loved making this meal for her family. And she was jittery, as usual, as her parents would be arriving any minute and as much as she tried, memories of Thanksgiving as a child ran through her. *Dad threw the turkey out the window because it was too dry,* she cringed. Every year Angela feared this, even though he was a changed man. "Baking relaxes me. But thanks Elyse."

Lexi came down the stairs, eyes looking wild.

Elyse ran to her. "Honey, what's wrong?"

"*Nothing.* Why?"

"It's Thanksgiving and you look kind of down."

Angela opened the oven and pointed to the bottom rack. "I made five pumpkin pies, and your favorite; pumpkin cheese pie."

Lexi's eyelids twitched. "Thanks, Angela."

Angela readjusting her red and white striped apron. "Nervous?"

Lexi nodded.

My dad scares the living daylights out of her, Angela thought, her mouth scrunched up to one side. Trying to distract Lexi, she asked "Have you made your shopping list for tomorrow?"

Lexi shrugged one shoulder. "Not really."

"Well," Angela said, "we'll just see what's out there and get ideas as we shop."

"Can Emma come?"

Envy ran through Angela, a rare happening. She'd wanted a special one-on-one time with Lexi. Her bond with Emma was something Angela couldn't seem to penetrate. Every attempt to go along with Lexi to Emma's to work on crafts, Lexi shot down. *Why?* "I don't think she can keep up," Angela finally said.

"Let's just go to small material shops. Get more stuff to make the Christmas hearts we're working on…"

"You know how much I love the big craft stores," Angela countered. Feeling daring, she said, "Maybe I can learn how to make those quilted hearts, too."

"Emma's living room's tiny."

Angela's heart sunk. "Well, I can help sell them then."

Lexi lit up. "We could take them to all the stores and ask them to put them in their windows."

"Good idea. Count me in." She snapped her fingers. "And I can sell them at the library."

"Would you?"

"I'm the librarian. I do have some say-so." The oven timer went off. "Just you and me tomorrow, alright? We'll make it our special day."

Lexi's face crimsoned but soon a smile slid across it. "Okay."

~*~

Lexi could take it no more. Angela's parents barely noticed their foster daughter. She wanted to yell, "Hello, I'm here, too." When they had to go around the table saying what they were thankful for, Grandpop, as she was told to call Angela's dad said, "His wonderful daughter and granddaughters." Nothing was said about her.

"I'm not feeling good," she told Angela. "Can I go lay

down?"

"Probably stuffed from the turkey," Grandpop said. "We'll all be napping soon."

The muscles in Angela's face tightened, a vein exposing itself across her forehead. She darted a look at her dad and then nodded. "You go ahead and lay down. Viruses going around."

"When I was a kid," Grandpop interjected, "we all got a whippin' if we didn't help clean up after a meal. No girls in the family, ya know."

Ali's jaw dropped. "Men can do dishes as well as us girls."

"Well, back in my day they didn't. Men are being sissified today, baking, cleaning house and –"

"Dad helps mom around the house," Ali continued. "Got up early to put the turkey on so mom could rest. You think he's a sissy?"

Grandpop snickered. "Maybe."

Lexi wanted to smack Grandpop for saying such a thing. She glanced quickly over at John and to her surprise, he squared his shoulders, opened his mouth, but then said nothing. Wasn't he going to stick up for himself? Angela didn't say anything either, only Ali defended her dad. "Sissy's don't work in coal mines, Grandpop."

"I agree," Grandmom said, slapping her husband on the arm.

Angela's eyes pooled with tears. "Dad, let's keep the conversation pleasant. It's a holiday."

Grandpop rolled his eyes. "Okay, Angela, my overly sensitive daughter."

"She's not being overly sensitive," John said evenly and then shot up, went over to the pies and held one up. "Anyone want my cherry pie? Picked the cherries and canned them myself."

"Oh, for Pete's sake," Grandpop snapped. "John, you've made your point."

"Want a piece?" John asked Grandpop with a hint of sarcasm in his voice.

"Ya, I'll try it. Made by a sis-"

"Benjamin, hush up!" Grandmom yelled. "Every Thanksgiving you act up. Why?"

Grandpop slowly lowered his head and then he looked up, sorrow filling his eyes. "Holidays bring back bad feelings."

"Such as?" Angela prodded.

"Not having a Thanksgiving as a kid. You know how my dad drank. No money for a good meal."

Angela nearly knocked her chair over as she sprang up and ran to her dad, throwing them around him from behind. "I'm sorry, Dad."

"Oh, it's me that's sorry." He looked over at John. "Sorry. Having a relapse I suppose."

"That's alright, Ben. Let's take a walk after dinner and talk about it." John rubbed his flat stomach. "Need to keep fit."

Tears fill Grandpop's eyes and Grandmom put a hand on his shoulder. Lexi wondered what this was all about. Still wanting to escape to her room, she asked again to be dismissed and Angela nodded.

~*~

Lexi clutched the antique looking red book Ali gave her. Having seen the movie and thinking it would be a boring book, she flipped though the pages at the sketches. The first one was Black Beauty grazing in a pasture with his mom. Lexi rolled her eyes. She'd never had a mom who spent more than two seconds near her. Never home, leaving her with her drunken dad.

Annoyed, she wanted to shut the book, but liking art, she went to the next sketch. *Birtwick Park*. Lexi remembered that this was Black Beauty's new home. *Beauty had to say good-bye to his mom*, she thought. When the social worker came to take her out of her home, her mother glared at her, yelling that she was a blabber-mouth. A razor-sharp pain rushed through her stomach, as it usually did when she replayed this event in her mind. Holding her middle, she breathed evenly until the pain subsided.

She wiped the perspiration from her forehead and dared to look at the next picture. Black Beauty was with Ginger running in a field. Her heart did a flip. Tricia was a friend like Ginger. And if she remembered right, Ginger was taken away from Black Beauty. The movie came back in high definition into her mind. Yes, Ginger and Merrylegs were well treated at Birtwick Park. Black Beauty learned to trust Joe, the boy who helped take care of the horses. And they were separated, too. The horse had many masters, some cruel, but Joe bought him after he was near-dead, providing a lasting home.

God, give me this, she prayed. *I'm afraid of where I might go next. What if I have to go home like Tricia?* And then she gasped. Why was she praying? Lexi didn't even believe in God. He never did her any favors.

I take it back. I don't need your help. I've had to defend myself since birth. You gave me a horrible home and so you're a horrible God if you're even real. Rage filled her and she threw the book against the wall, breaking the spine. *Ali will kill me!* Running to retrieve the book, she examined the damage. Glue. She'd buy glue tomorrow when she went shopping with Angela.

She took a deep breath. Her social worker and Angela had helped her with her temper. But would she ever control it? Grandpop was near a hundred years old and he still thought back to hard memories and snapped. Lexi buried her head in her pillow and screamed, hoping no one could hear. And then she let the tears flow. Emma said it was good to cry. Emma cried. Emma understood her somehow.

~*~

Angela jumped up and down to keep warm. "Only five more minutes."

"More people than last year," Lexi said, blowing warm air into her mittens.

Snowflakes began to fall and Angela stuck out her tongue to catch one. "Try it," she said.

Angela confused Lexi. Her dad made her nervous yesterday but today she was like a kid. Wanting answers, she said, "Grandpop sure was a grump yesterday."

"You think so?" Angela asked, collecting another snowflake on her tongue.

Lexi's eyes widened. "Yes, don't you?"

"Oh, he's come a long way. And he's so sorry for everything."

"What did he do?" Lexi wondered.

Angela hugged herself as she shivered. "He was an alcoholic and has lots of regrets."

"Did he ever hit you or throw you across the room? Ever break a bone?" Lexi blurted.

"No broken bones, but yes, I was thrown around." She slammed her eyes shut. "Landed on a glass coffee table once and it shattered. Mom was so mad."

"That you were hurt or the coffee table got smashed?"

"That he threw me," Angela said, her voice shaky. "My

mom snapped, so tired of living in a dysfunctional family and she made Dad get help." Angela strained to smile. "Dad has relapses, but he's pretty normal now, and mom's happy."

Lexi was numb. She'd imagined Angela's life to be so perfect.

"So glad I met John when I did…." Angela said, putting a hand to her heart.

"How old were you?"

"Sixteen. He lived down the road and the whole neighborhood knew about my dad's rages. Sometimes I ran to his house."

Really? Lexi couldn't imagine Angela so young, let alone not in a perfect world.

A shadow cast over Angela's pretty eyes. "Lexi, my dad wasn't himself when drunk. Alcohol, if taken too much is like being addicted to drugs." She shifted. "Dad went to Alcoholics Anonymous, admitted he had a problem and found God."

"Found God?"

"Yes. It's one of the steps in AA. You have to find something higher than yourself and mom gave him a Bible. He read it faithfully and could relate to James and John being called 'Sons of Thunder.'"

"What's that mean?" Lexi asked, still not able to take all this in.

"James and John were followers of Jesus who had bad

tempers. Jesus nicknamed them Sons of Thunder. When Dad realized Jesus didn't judge them, but met them where they were, he asked Jesus to do the same for him."

Lexi thought of her dad's rages and it seemed unfair that Jesus would forgive such a terrible person. "Angela, do you think Jesus should forgive my dad? And my mom for not stopping things?"

Angela stroked Lexi's cheek. "If he asks for forgiveness, yes, but God is also fair. He's love and justice combined. He said if anyone hurts a child it would be better for them to have a stone thrown around their neck and tossed into the sea. Pretty strong words."

Lexi grabbed Angela's hand. "Your dad threw you into a coffee table. Why did God forgive him?"

"Because he asked. He admitted he needed help. Jesus came for people who want help." She looked pensively at her boots. "I prayed for my dad because I knew deep down he was just mad at his dad. That's what he was talking about yesterday. My grandfather was a violent drunk and the holidays can bring back bad memories to my dad sometimes."

Lexi hugged Angela. "I love you. We both had it rough, huh?"

"Yes."

"I never want to forgive my dad," Lexi insisted, pulling away, embarrassed that she displayed such emotion in a crowded parking lot.

A whistle was heard announcing the store was open for business. The crowd pressed in hard and a man behind Lexi pushed her and she panicked. Would she get trampled like they showed on TV? "Angela, help!"

Angela took her hand, glaring at the man. "Stop it. You're crushing my daughter."

"Got a problem, lady?"

"Yes, I do," Angela yelled. "My daughter's getting hurt. Now step back you big…ape!"

"Go home if you can't take the crowds, lady."

Angela pulled Lexi to her, hovering over her like a protective mama bear. Panting, Angela asked Lexi if she was alright. "You called me your daughter," Lexi beamed.

"I was afraid. I love you, honey. People can get trampled to death."

Lexi began to laugh. "Angela, you sure told that guy off. Called him an ape."

"I know. I couldn't help it. He was acting like an animal."

Lexi stared at Angela not knowing what to say, until Angela burst into laughter. Lexi laughed, too, nervous laughter mixed with joy. She'd felt protected by a mom. What a wonderful feeling.

Chapter 4

Jinxed?

Snow pelted against Emma's little dawdyhaus the next day, and she hugged herself around the middle. The memory of Atley holding her tight, warming her on their first sleigh ride as a married couple overpowered her. Her eyes stung as tears threatened to pour, but she knew Lexi would be over in a few minutes and the dear girl needed her to be strong. Truth be told, she needed Lexi. Her grandkinner were all a happy bunch, all eighty-some of them, but Lexi needed her. She needed to be needed. Such an empty hole Atley left in her heart.

I love your pumpkin pancakes. Can you make me a stack high?

This sock has a hole in it. Can you mend it?

Picked you lots of apples. Can you make more apple butter?

Emma shook her head, trying to dislodge memories of Atley. *Lord, help me. Is it the holidays that make me miss him so?*

A tear slid down her cheek as she stared at the cross-stitching on the red gingham heart. *Love.* Another tear and then another...

Cold air rushed at Emma and she darted her gaze up. "Lexi!

Ach, you startled me."

Lexi ran and knelt before her, boots dripping water all over her hardwood floors. "Why are you crying?"

She could not add to this little girl's problems. "Maybe coming down with a cold."

"A cold doesn't make you cry, Emma. What's wrong? Didn't you have good sales yesterday?"

Grabbing a handkerchief from her apron pocket she dabbed her eyes. "*Jah*. Black Friday was *gut*. Sold the white quilt."

"For the asking price?"

"*Jah*, for eight-hundred."

"Good," Lexi said. "Sometimes the English try to get people to lower prices." She put a hand on her hip. "Your handkerchief has Atley's name on it. Why?"

Emma slipped it back into her pocket. "I made it for him. I use it now. Miss him."

"Ew," Lexi grimaced.

"I soaked it in soap and then boiled it. Handkerchiefs can be heirloom gifts, handed down from generation to generation."

Lexi's face twist in disgust. "I'd rather have a new one." Lifting up a bag, Lexi said, "Guess what I bought yesterday."

Emma could tell by the shape of the bag it was a bolt of material. "Let's see. Leftover autumn colored fabric on clearance?"

"Nope." She drew up red and green calico material. "A

dollar a yard. Angela and I hit the jackpot. We got ten of them!"

Emma was amazed at the glow on Lexi's face. "Well, that'll make our profit margin near eighty percent, *jah*?"

"Ya, and we got bags of stuffing for the hearts, too. And Angela said she'd sell hearts at the library and go around all the stores in Smicksburg to see if they'll sell them."

"Make a window display?"

"Yes."

"So the town theme can be….love." Emma turned her work in progress around, revealing what she was cross-stitching.

Lexi narrowed her eyes. "*Love*. It looks nice. Can you teach me how to cross-stitch like that?"

"You're good at art. Just write the word out with a tracing pencil, very light so you can barely see it, and cross-stitch over it." Emma reached into her basket full of pre-cut hearts. "Here, what will you put on it?"

Lexi bit her lower lip. "I don't know."

"Well, faith, hope and love will always remain, the Bible says. How about hope?"

Lexi's shoulders drooped. "Alright."

"What's wrong?

Lexi took a needle and green embroidery thread from Emma sewing basket. "I don't have any."

"*Ach*, child, no hope? At your age?"

"Well, I have to be careful. I've been hopeful before about lots of stuff but…"

"It doesn't happen?" Emma probed.

"Yes."

Emma didn't know whether to prod deeper, but she did, moved with compassion for this dear girl. "What didn't happen?"

Lexi took a tracing pencil and started to write hope on a material heart. "You know, Emma."

"I think I do, but it helps to talk about things…"

"I hope never to go back and live with my parents and live in Smicksburg my whole life. There, I said it, now it won't happen. I'm jinxed."

Jinxed? What on earth? "Lexi, there's no such thing as being jinxed."

"Okay, unlucky."

"No such thing as that, either."

"How do you know? Some people have it harder than others." She slowly put her pencil down. "Did you know Angela was jinxed until she met John?"

Emma wanted to stop all this silly talk, but Lexi's face was so earnest. "What do you mean?"

"Angela was abused like me. Well, not as bad, but her dad was a drunk and mean. John helped her. It's like a fairytale, the prince coming to save his princess."

Emma coughed to hide a chuckle. "Really? No one helped Angela but John?"

Lexi leaned back in the rocker. "She said other neighbors helped."

"*Ach*, so she was helped in community."

"What?"

"We get help by the Lord above and others near us. We can't attach all our praise to one person for saving us. *Nee*, we need to reach out to our neighbors and family."

"So why do you cry by yourself?" Lexi asked softly.

I'm going through a grief no one can share, only the Lord. It's something a whole community can't take away."

"But they can help," Lexi said, determined. "How come your grandkids don't visit you more?"

"They do…"

"When?"

Emma felt fatigue wash over her. "Only Marie's *kinner* live nearby over in the farmhouse."

"But I never see them over here…"

Emma tried to not speak in haste, but measure her words. "They know you're here."

Lexi gasped. "And they don't want to talk to an *Englisher*?"

"*Nee*, it's not that."

"Then what is it?"

Emma reached over for Lexi's hand, but she drew back.

Heartsick, Emma had to confess. "You cussed, smoked and stole when you first came to Angela and John's. Marie thought you were a bad influence."

"But I don't do that anymore."

"I know. Marie talked to Angela about it yesterday at the quilt shop. Maria admitted she can trust you."

"Trust me? Angela said that?" Lexi asked.

"*Jah*. Be a Trusted English Friend, like Angela and John. We have to test folks before we get too close. Some are bad apples and can ruin the whole bushel. Marie's a little stricter since her son left the Amish after being with a bad apple."

Lexi brightened. "So Marie likes me?"

"*Jah*, she does. And we'd be happy to have you around more. Maybe learn to milk goats and brush down horses?"

"I'd like to work with horses. I'm reading *Black Beauty*. Horses have feeling like us humans. They can feel pain."

Emma rejoiced. Lexi was opening up like her white tulips in spring. The more she stopped shutting down her emotions, the more the Lord could heal her…in community.

~*~

Sunday night, Lexi watched from her bedroom window as Angela walked her daughters to their cars. *All three linked together*, Lexi fussed. She was a fool to think Angela had real motherly feelings for her. A pit lodged itself in her stomach. As Ali and Elyse were headed back to college, she would have to go to the 'prison' of school. Amish kids had it so easy, only going to eighth grade.

As the cars pulled out, Angela waved and then oddly looked up at her window. Lexi moved back until Angela had returned to the house. Then she looked out at the cloudless night. It was filled with stars and as usual, an eerie feeling crept over her. The stars didn't touch each other. They were alone, out in space, isolated for life. Why John liked to watch the stars was a mystery to her. Seemed so stupid.

Stupid. She flung herself on her bed. How could she endure school without Tricia to stick up for her when the kids called her stupid? *DeLexi Lexi,* they taunted, saying she must see things backwards like she was dyslexic since she stuttered when she read aloud

A lone howl pierced the night. *Poor Sebatian,* she thought. The dog was tied up too much. Couldn't the Barton's let the dog in on a cold night? But another howl, and then a whimper. Lexi shot up and dashed to the window. Out in the snow was the form of a dog. Lexi struggled to lift the window and was soon dangling out of it. "Hey, boy, you okay?" she asked. The dog barked and whimpered again and then lay in the snow, head on the ground. Was it hurt?

Lexi ran to retrieve her robe and slippers and made her way down the hall and then steps without being seen. She slowly opened the door, and stood on the front porch. "Are you friendly?"

The dog stood as if frozen, all but its tail that wagged like a flag.

Lexi dismounted four steps and the dog knocked her back, lathered her with a kiss. This huge saliva machine had his paws on her shoulders, pinning her down to the steps. "Stop it," she griped. He darted away, tail between his legs.

"Stop. I won't hurt you," she said to the cowering dog. She ran to him, pet his matted fur, and she noticed chunks were missing. She rubbed his back but when she pressed on one spot the dog whimpered. "You're hurt, poor thing."

A blast of cold air whirled around Lexi and then the snow started to fly. "I can't leave you out here." She reached for a collar to see if there was a name tag and felt something round and cold. *Someone owned this dog?* She wanted to scream. How could anyone hurt such a sweet dog?

Lexi paced the ground, her moccasins getting damp. She missed Tricia. *She'd know what to do. What would Tricia do?* she wondered. Lexi looked up at the full moon and then grabbed the dog by the collar and led him towards the house. She peeked in and saw Angela back in her kitchen and John was nowhere to be seen. "Now be quiet, boy," she whispered. "I'll hide you in my room for tonight, and then I'll sneak you over to Emma's."

She ran up the stairs, the dog panting behind. When

reaching her room, she turned on the lights and the dog jumped on her bed. Lexi saw there were little wounds everywhere. "Boy, are you okay? Are you hungry?" The dog sat up and appeared to be begging her for food. "Well, you look starved." She lay next to him and decided she'd sneak some food out of the refrigerator when everyone was asleep. She'd protect…this big dog. "You're a White Beauty," she whispered in his ear. "I'll protect you, like Joe protected Black Beauty."

She ran to her desk to grab the book, and upon opening it, she was relieved that her glue job had fixed the spine. Lexi snuggled up to White Beauty, and by the glow of her flashlight, read the book until she dozed-off.

~*~

A loud bang echoed from the chamber of the long pistol, but Lexi stood between the bullet and the white dog. She would protect him.

"Lexi, wake up! Why is your door locked?" Angela yelled, knocking on the door. "You'll miss the bus again!"

Pushing herself off the floor, Lexi prepared herself for battle. She shook her head. *She was dreaming? Was the dog a dream?* She twirled around and saliva bathed her face. *Ew!* Hugging him around the neck, she felt slumber lift.

"Lexi, open the door!"

"Angela…I think I'm sick."

"Lexi, we've been over this. You've missed too much

school. No more fibbing."

"I'm not lying." She sprung up and paced the room, wondering which illness she could pick from the vast collection of scenarios in her mind. Itchiness soon overtook her and little red dots caught her attention. They were up and down her arms. "I have a rash," she lied. Lexi knew a flea bite when she saw it.

"Let me in. I want to see it."

"I'll come down to the kitchen…"

"Why?"

"I, ah…"

"What?"

"I started your Christmas present and you'll see it if you come in," she spit out in rapid succession.

"Oh. Meet me downstairs in a few minutes, and I mean *few*, not half an hour so you miss the bus on purpose again."

When she heard Angela's footsteps on the stairs, she ran to get her pajamas on. If there was ever a time she wished for a bathroom off her room, it was now. She reeked of wet dog. Raking a comb through her hair, she went over to the snoozing dog and rubbed his neck. "Stay here." He opened one eye and then closed it. "You're exhausted White Beauty. Or stuffed from all the food you ate." She smiled and she stroked the dog more. Love poured out of her heart for this dog and memories raced through her mind of the dog that protected her. Mr.

Beech's collie ran over to check on her. When her dad went into a rage, the dog ran over and would bark up a storm, making the neighbors all wonder what was going on, making her dad close his mouth. Lexi kissed the dog. "You stay here."

Lexi heard Angela call again and she sprinted across the room and down the steps.

"Pretty peppy for someone sick."

Lexi hated lying to Angela, but today it was for a good reason. She needed to save her dog. Exposing her arms, she pointed to the rash.

Angela came nearer but stepped back. "Oh, you stink!"

"I'm sorry. Maybe it's the infection."

"You smell like wet dog fur."

"I do? People smell funny when they're sick." Lexi pulled up her pajama pant legs revealing her calves. "See, the rash is everywhere."

Angela pinched her nose and looked closely at the red dots. "How odd. Have you ever had chicken pocks?"

"I don't know."

As Angela stared in disbelief, Lexi made her story bigger. "I forgot to tell you. Mrs. McAllister said that a rare virus was going around the class. I think she said chicken pox. Actually, I'm sure she did. How could I forget?"

Angela glanced at her watch. "I have to go to work. John worked last night and is sleeping. He can take you to the

43

doctors when he gets up."

Not wanting John to take her to the doctor, she blurted, "I'm okay."

"You are not. Now, go take a shower and get some fresh pajamas on."

Chapter 5

A Stray Dog

Lexi squirmed as she sat next to John in the waiting room. He insisted going in with her? What if the doctor had to check this 'rash' everywhere? "I want to see the doctor by myself," she said evenly.

"I have some questions for him."

Inhaling to keep calm, she continued. "I have privacy rights."

"When you're eighteen. For now I'm your dad." He leaned towards her. "It'll be okay. My questions don't have anything to do with your flea bites."

She glowered. "Fleas? What?"

"Lexi. Where'd you get them?"

Gulp. She scrambled for words. "Emma. She has cats."

"You smell like a wet dog."

"Fur is fur."

"I know. I hunt and they all smell different. Now, fess up."

Crossing her arms, she turned to him, squaring her shoulders. "It was Emma's dog then. I don't know."

"Well, maybe you're sick because you ate half the refrigerator."

Lexi knew John would return White Beauty to its owner. He always did what was so-called 'right'. No, she would hold to her story. "Emma's dogs really smell. I, ah, have to confess something."

"I'm all ears."

"I heard a dog crying outside last night, around midnight. I opened the window to see that Emma's dog got loose. It was crying outside my window because he wanted me. Didn't you hear him?"

John smirked. "Oh, yes I did. Angela woke me up. We saw Ole' Boy but figured since he was 'crying' right under *your* window, he missed you, not us."

"Really?"

"Oh, yes. Animals just *love* you and you *love* them, right?"

"Yes,' she said, heart banging.

"Good, because I've been thinking…"

"And?"

"Well, you said Emma called you a Trusted English Friend, right?"

"So?"

"She needs help cleaning out animal pens. You know the mess animals leave behind."

Wanting to slap John, she growled. "I'm not cleaning up

manure."

"Oh yes you are…unless you tell me the truth." He slowly put up a hand. "If you need help, don't be afraid to ask instead of making up wild stories."

If you need help, don't be afraid to ask… Lexi pondered these words. She'd never heard them from a man. She saw compassion on John's face and it disarmed her. "Okay."

"So what's going on?"

"A stray dog. It *was* crying outside my window. I let it in last night, fed it." Mustering up her courage, she stated firmly, "And I won't let the mean man who owned White take him back."

"What mean man?" John asked, jaw dropping. "The dog looks abused?"

Now the stone wall erected between them had a crack. "Yes. Bruised, missing hair, and skinny. I fed him. And I hid him."

"Where is he now?"

"In my room…"

John let out a long whistle that meant 'oh no', but then said a shocking thing. "I'll help you but Angela will not be happy. She's afraid of dogs and is a clean freak. That's why there are no animals in the house."

Lexi blinked rapidly in disbelief. "Really?"

"I've wanted a dog for years but won't chain one outside.

Maybe this dog was sent to us."

"His name is White Beauty," Lexi said, leaning closer to John. "I'm reading Black Beauty and changed the color."

John put an arm around her. "You're reading Black Beauty? I love that book. I gave my leather copy to Ali . Passed down from my grandpa."

The nurse called t for them and they made their way into the doctor's office. Doc Adams entered, making Lexi feel anxious since he was a huge man, like her dad. "So, what do we have here?"

John spoke up. "Hi Doc. Lexi's just tagging along to keep me company."

"Really? But it's a school day."

John eyed the doctor. "I thought it would benefit her. I wanted to talk to you about S.A.D. Working down in the mines, I see no sunlight and I dread these next few months. February's the worst."

Doc Adams cleared his throat, appearing a little confused. "Seasonal Affective Disorder can make you tired, sad, feeling trapped. A whole host of symptoms. Does Lexi have these symptoms, too?

Lexi shook her head as she clenched her sweaty palms.

"Well, she looks tired sometimes," John said.

Doc Adams readjusted his wire-rimmed glasses. "Depressed at all?"

"No," John said, "can't say I'm depressed, just tired. Angela says I can get a little edgy. I feel antsy at times, like I want to jump out of my skin."

"That would be anxiety then. Ever think of hurting yourself?" Doc Adams asked.

"No," John said. "How about you, Lexi? Are you dealing with any of this?"

"No," Lexi lied, meeting John's big brown eyes. John felt like she did? *Anxious? Wanting to jump out of his skin? Yes!*

Doc Adams pursed his lips. "John, are you depressed that Tricia had to go back to her parents?"

He nodded. "Maybe I'm worried about her. Her future and all." He glanced toward Lexi and then said, "But I'm like this every winter."

"Well, lack of sunlight can be hard on the nerves. Vitamin D is in sunlight and your body needs it to absorb needed minerals. I'll start you on a higher dose of D and magnesium. See you in a week. We'll talk *privately* then.

"Young Lady," Doc Adams said, "I've noticed something. You have a rash on your neck."

He moved towards her and she panicked. "Flea bites. I got a new dog. John and I did." She begged John with her eyes to take it from there, which he did.

"Ya, Doc, a stray came by and Lexi and I got bit up." John lifted his shirt sleeve to reveal flea bites." Called an

49

exterminator this morning."

"That can be expensive," Doc said.

John winked at Lexi. "He's worth it."

Lexi felt that somehow John wasn't talking about the dog at all, but her. A ray of hope beamed into her heart, but then a thud. *No*, she chided herself. *Don't get your hopes up.* I'm just another foster kid that John pities just like the dog.

~*~

"John, get this dog out of here!" Angela screamed, perched on a kitchen chair.

"Here White," John said.

"White? John, the dogs all dirty and it's gross."

Lexi wanted to sink into non-existence. Disappear. Be invisible. She'd never seen Angela so angry.

"Honey," John said, taking the dog by the collar, "Lexi found the dog and tried to help."

Angela stomped a foot, making the wooden chair shake. "It was on the counter! Tipped over a canister of flour and ate it."

"It's starving, honey" He turned to Lexi. "Here, take White."

"It's White Beauty," Lexi corrected.

"Let's call him White for short," he said evenly. Going to his wife, he helped her off the chair. "This dog won't bite you."

Angela flung out her arms. "I'm all bit up. Fleas I suppose. Lexi's so-called rash." She darted a glare at Lexi. "You lied again."

"It *is* a rash. I *flea* rash. How was I supposed to know?"

"Lexi," John said, "remember, you can talk to us, okay?"

"Alright, I did lie but it was for a good cause. I needed to save this dog."

"Lexi," Angela exclaimed, "two wrongs don't make a right. It's never right to lie, even if it's for a good reason."

John massaged Angela's shoulders. "Sweetheart, I called an exterminator. He should be here by the end of the day."

"And that costs a lot, right around the holidays."

"And Lexi and I have a job to pay for it."

Angela's eyes softened. "Together?"

"Yes, we're going to clean animal stalls and shovel snow for Amish widows who need help."

"Claire Shlaubaugh needs help."

"We'll get word out. Lexi won't go unpunished for what she did." Turning to her, he said, "Lexi, you understand, right?"

Lexi oddly did understand and nodded.

Angela slouched and then opened her arms, the sign to come give her a hug. "You're forgiven."

Lexi ran into her arms. "Can we keep White?"

"I'm afraid of dogs, Lexi. I'm a cat person."

"Not me," John grimaced. "First things first, though. We need to find the owner. If it was abused, it needs reported. Until then, we should nurse him back to health."

Angela chewed on her bottom lip. "I won't sleep a wink."

John put his arms around Angela and Lexi. "I'll protect my women-folk," he laughed.

I'm not afraid, Lexi thought. *But it sure feels nice to hear someone will protect me.*

Chapter 6

White Beauty

Lexi endured the next day at school without Tricia, but barely. No one understood about being a foster kid and she had to rehash over and over that it was a temporary home and Tricia's parents got her back. The question that followed was always, *Will you go back and live with your parents, too?* She knew lying was wrong but said her parents were living in Europe, in France, and she had to stay behind because she couldn't speak French. What else could she say? The truth? No, Jimmy Falco would poke fun to no end, and he'd be merciless if he knew the truth.

Hopping off the bus, she zipped up her jacket and started plunging through the snow a few blocks to her house. As she got nearer, she narrowed her eyes. Was she dreaming? Angela was walking White down the road to meet her? She ran towards her and noticed the fear in Angela's eyes. "Hi. What are you doing?"

"I promised John I'd try to like the dog."

"Why?"

"He wants to keep him. Well, after the investigation and if no one claims him."

"Investigation?"

"The dog tag had a name and address. John went to the animal shelter in Punxsy and they're trying to find the owner."

Lexi rubbed White's back gently. "No dog should have bruises like this. Look, his fur is pink in spots, stained by blood."

"John told the vet to give him as gentle a flea bath as possible." Angela held out the leash. "I'll take that backpack of yours and you take White." She pursed her lips, trying to hide a smile. "Marie stopped by this morning, asking if I could go with you to Emma's to make Christmas hearts. Supper's in the Crock-pot, so let's walk over."

Resentment crammed Lexi's heart. Marie didn't trust her like she said. Or was it her husband, Levi? Angela was only there to keep her in line. Most likely the whole town knew about White and what a liar she was. Shaking her head to dislodge this thought, she looked up at Angela. "You're brave, Angela. And it's a nice thing you're doing for John, too."

"Honey, John wants me to overcome my fears," she grumbled. "But I can't sleep with that dog in the house. Tired all day."

"But he needs a home."

"Well, it may not be ours." A frosty mist wafted from her

lips. "So, how was school?"

Lexi could hardly keep White from dragging her. Pulling back on the leash she said, "I hate it."

"Why?"

"Wish I was homeschooled like Abby at church. She never has to get up early."

"Is that the only reason?"

"Well," Lexi continued, "I go to one class and love it, like art, but as soon as I really get into my project, the bell rings and I have to go to math or science."

"So you're saying you can learn better by doing one thing for longer times?"

Lexi and Angela turned to walk down the long driveway to Emma's *dawdyhaus*. "I guess so. Emma taught me to sew and do all kinds of crafts. It took me hours at a time to learn to do satin-stitch, but I learned it. Abby's so lucky."

"Well, you know foster parents can't home school in this state. But there's always a bend in the road."

Lexi stopped, making White jerk back on his leash. "What's that mean? Am I leaving like Tricia?"

Angela looked away, as if admiring the winter scenery. "I hope not. I don't think so."

Fear darted through Lexi's heart. Something was wrong. Angela had information and it was making her nervous.

As they approached Emma's little house next to the main

farmhouse that Marie, her youngest daughter lived in, along with eight children, and jealousy ran through Lexi. *Must be nice to have a perfect life.* What she wouldn't give to be a part of this family.

"Hello," Emma yelled as she leaned on her snow shovel.

Angela returned the greeting but Lexi just gasped and ran with White to Emma. "You're too old to shovel snow."

"It's for you to do," she quipped. "Nice thing you and John are doing for widows. He put a sign up in the shop." Emma bent over to pet the dog. "Who's this?"

"A stray dog we found," Lexi mumbled, wondering why John had to advertise their snow shoveling business. "Did John's sign say anything about shoveling manure?"

Emma tilted her head. "No, just snow. Why?"

Relief swept through Lexi along with gratitude. "Just wondering."

Emma knelt down to eye White. "*Ach*, the poor boy. He's skinny. Let's get him some cream right from the cow."

"Seriously?" Angela asked.

"Well, not right from the cow, but I have some I'm going to make butter with. Price of butter at Punxsy-Mart is a dollar a stick."

"We can't take your cream," Angela said.

"Well, there's plenty where that comes from." She turned to Lexi. "And since you're going to be helping out around her

56

and getting to know my *grandkinner*, maybe you can help get more milk."

"Milk a cow?" Lexi huffed. "I don't know how."

"Ida does. And she's coming over to help make hearts. You can get to know each other since Marie's finally letting her *kinner* befriend more *Englishers.*" She rose and pat Angela's shoulder. "You and John paved the way, you know. First your family, now half your church can be trusted."

"They're good people," Angela offered. "Not perfect, though."

"Just like us Amish." Emma leaned the shovel against the porch rail. "Lexi, you can do this later. Come in and get warmed up. Hot chocolate's on the stove."

"Can I bring White in?"

"*Jah*, as long as he sits still."

Angela clucked her tongue and Lexi squeezed her hand. "He's not dangerous."

When they went into the little living room, Lexi could smell pine and then she saw boughs of pine branches lining the window sills. "I thought the Amish didn't decorate for Christmas."

"No Christmas trees, but we can put up greens and whatnot."

"Why no Christmas trees?" Lexi asked, intrigued by Amish ways.

Emma poured two mugs of hot chocolate from her speckleware pot and placed them on the coffee table. "Well, Lexi, we keep it simple."

"Do you think they're bad?" Lexi continued.

Emma grinned. "Well, they're fancy. We stick to plain."

"So how can you sell Christmas ornaments for trees?" Lexi asked.

"Too many questions, Lexi," Angela said firmly.

Lexi always said whatever was on her mind at Emma's. *Would Angela ruin it all?*

Emma poured a glass jar of cream into a bowl and placed it in front of White and the dog began to lap noisily. She took her usual place at her rocker and glanced at Angela. "Lexi can ask me anything. I don't mind. We Amish have little ornaments like the hearts that we hang in our windows or give as little presents. Remember Atley's beeswax hearts?"

"Scented with cinnamon," Angela added. "They were unique presents."

Angela frowned. "I wonder if I got the idea for the hearts from Atley making them. *Ach*, I do miss him something fierce."

"We pray for you," Angela said. "Grief is hard, especially around Christmas."

"*Jah*. We exchanged presents, you know. Last year he got me a down filled lap quilt. Now I keep warm in bed with it since he's not here to snuggle up to."

Angela glanced over at White. "So you need companionship and warmth?"

"*Jah*, maybe."

"How much land do you have?"

"All together, eighty acres, I think. Why?"

Angela cleared her throat. "Lexi, don't you think White would be happier here with all the land to run around on? We live in town with a small yard."

"B-But John wants a dog," Lexi sputtered.

"I'm sorry. Just being in the same room as that dog makes my heart thump. He's could rip my leg off in one bite."

"He wouldn't hurt a fly," Emma said. "You can tell. His tail's wagging. Not aggressive at all."

"I know. But I just can't do this," Angela said, wiping sweat from her forehead. "We all have things we fear and for me, it's big dogs."

"But Angela, you said you'd try," Lexi cried. "We need to get White better."

Emma put up a hand. "He can stay here on the farm. I can't say I'd want him on my bed for warmth or whatnot, but he's made to run, looks part Shepherd."

"No he doesn't. German Shepherds aren't white," Lexi said, agitated.

"*Ach*, there's all kinds of shepherds." Emma observed White closer. "He may even have a dash of Husky in him."

"He looks part wolf," Angela said, eyes wide.

Lexi gripped the leash tight. "God hasn't given us a spirit of fear."

Emma gasped. "Lexi, you're memorizing the verses I suggested."

Lexi nodded. "Angela, you should memorize that verse, too."

Angela leaned her head back on the rocker, appearing weak. "I know it. God has not given us a spirit of fear, but of power, love and a sound mind."

Lexi's eyes bugged out. "That was good. And it's in 2 Timothy 1:7. Timothy was scared of lots of things and Paul told him he needed to stop being such a chicken."

Emma laughed out loud. "Now, that's a hint if I ever did hear one."

Angela rolled her eyes. "Alright, I'll practice what I preach. That was last weeks Sunday school lesson."

Lexi wanted to do a cartwheel across the room. "Thanks, Angela."

The door opened, letting in a few snowflakes. Ida, a girl Lexi often said hello to while going to Emma's appeared. She had reddish hair peeking though her white prayer kapp. Freckles were sprinkled over her nose and cheeks. This girl ran to the dog and scratched White behind the ears. "*Oma*, is this for you?" And then she froze. "I'm sorry. Hi Angela, Lexi."

"Nee, it's the Stotlers' dog." Emma looked up over her wire rimmed glasses at Angela. "John loves dogs. He said he wanted to learn more about farm animals? Are you planning on buying up one of the farms for sale?"

Angela gasped. "John likes dogs but I don't see him being a real farmer."

"He gets depressed being down in the coal mine," Lexi said. "Can't see the sun all winter."

A smile graced Angela's pretty face. "He shared that with you? I'm glad you and John have become chatterboxes all of a sudden, but I smell mischief…"

"John wants to live off the land, more." Lexi said. "I think he's trapped in a farmer's body."

"I can teach him all he needs to know, along with my *bruder*. I could never live without animals to tend to. They calm me," Ida said, hands in her apron pockets swaying. "Poor John that he has to live in the dark."

"Ida, would you like to sit down and help with the hearts?" Emma asked.

"*Ach,* Oma, I came so you could listen to the song I'm singing in the Christmas program at school. But I can come back."

"We'd love to hear it and it would give you practice singing in front of other people. Go on, Ida," Emma encouraged.

Ida's freckles paled as she blushed. "Do I have to?"

"*Nee*, only if you want to."

Ida glanced at them all, and then said, "Teacher says to never be nervous in front of friends. So I'll sing it, but if I mess up, don't laugh."

"We won't," Angela assured her.

Ida pulled out a piece of paper from her pocket and began to sing:

Love came down at Christmas,
Love all lovely, Love Divine,
Love was born at Christmas,
Stars and Angels gave the sign.

Worship we the Godhead
Love incarnate, love divine
Worship we our Jesus
But wherewith for sacred sign?

Love shall be our token,
Small gift until something greater is given
Love shall be yours and love be mine,
Love to God and all men,
Love for plea and gift and sign.

Angela clapped vigorously. "I love that song. I hear it on the radio."

"You sing real good," Lexi said.

Emma's eyes beamed with love for her granddaughter. "I sang that song when I was a youth."

"Is it old then?" Angela asked. "I thought it was a contemporary Christian song."

"It's as old as the hills," Emma said.

Ida sat next to White. "*Jah, Oma*, the words are old. What does, 'Love shall be our token' mean?"

Emma picked up a heart and needle and resumed her work. "It explains it in the song. A small gift. We can't pay God enough for coming into this fallen world on Christmas, all we can offer are little gifts. Like A token is a small gift, *jah*? And the greatest gift we can give is to love God and others."

"That's the song we'll sing for Light-Up-Night," Angela said, snapping her fingers. "It's easy and the real message of Christmas is in it." She met Lexi's eyes. "Do you think it's the right song? Want to help me with the kid's choir?"

Lexi just stared. Fears of leaving soon just lifted. Angela was saying she'd be with them on Christmas…no need to fear…for now.

Chapter 7

∽

Be Amish!

After a few nights of restless sleep, Angela confessed she could not live with White in her house. "I talked to Emma and she'll take him."

"But, you said we need to face our fears," Lexi challenged over breakfast.

"We do, but I also need sleep. Maybe we can get a pet rabbit, a Flemish Giant. I've always wanted one. They're as big as a dog."

John dashed salt across his eggs. "Really? Me, too." He turned to Lexi. "How about it?"

Lexi swallowed the lump forming in her throat. "I love dogs."

"You can teach a rabbit all kinds of stuff," Angela said. "Over at Smicksburg Pottery, Roosevelt hops over to customers to give them their receipt."

Lexi wanted to scream, 'boring' but held her tongue, trying to think before speaking. "Can we keep White outside in a doghouse?"

"I don't think that's a life for a dog," John said. "He'd be mighty cold."

"Can he stay in the garage?" Lexi persisted.

"No one's here all day to let him out." Angela looked earnestly at Lexi. "Sometimes when God closes a door, he opens a window."

"To jump out of?" Lexi blurted, not able to control herself.

John's face grew red and then burst into laughter. "Funny, Lexi."

"Really?" Lexi asked. "She was beginning to actually like John lately. Lexi jabbed a piece of bacon. "When I grow up, I'm going to be a dog breeder."

John slouched. "When I grow up I want to be a farmer." He winked at Angela.

"So I hear. Lexi told us over at Emma's. John, are you serious?"

"No. I have to do the work that's here and that's down in the mines."

"Honey, I know you feel trapped," Angela persisted. "What kind of farm?"

"A hobby farm is what I'd like. Five acres with all that we'd need to homestead. Live off the land, grow our own food."

Lexi wished she could live in Smicksburg forever with either the Stotlers or over at Emma's. Country living took her by surprise, making her feel calmer."

"Are you taking your Vitamin D?" Angela asked John. "You always feel too cooped up this time of year."

"Yes. Maybe I need a higher dose," John said. "But being outside is half the battle with the winter blues. Lexi, don't forget about the church meeting tonight. We'll take Joseph outside and fix him there."

"But I wanted to work over at Emma's to make hearts."

"And she needs to study," Angela added.

"Lexi, see how much more time you have since we threw the TV out?" John smirked. "You can go to Emma's after school and then we'll head over to the church after dinner."

"And homework?" Angela crowed.

"Ida can help me over at Emma's," Lexi said. "She's good at math."

"But you'll be making hearts," Angela said, one eyebrow cocked.

"I'll take breaks from making hearts to do math with Ida. Okay?"

"Okay," Angela agreed. "And you can take White over when you go."

"No ones claimed him yet," John said in a faraway voice. "The address on his collar is an abandoned house. Poor boy. I wonder if he lived in the house without food and water and escaped. Some people are cruel to animals…"

"White needs love now more than ever," Lexi begged,

staring at Angela.

Angela slowly closed her eyes. "Okay, I'll try one more night. But if I can't sleep, White goes tomorrow."

~*~

Lexi ran down the path to Emma's as White pulled her along. "Whoa, boy."

Trying to balance the weight of her backpack full of homework, she felt ice under the snow and slid. "White! Slow down!"

The dog turned, cocked an ear and then slowed his pace.

"Hey, that was good. Can you sit?"

He put his butt on the cold ground.

"Roll over?"

He lay down, spun on his back and then lifted his paws as if wanting something.

"You want a treat! Someone's trained you." She scratched behind his ears and felt his fur seemed thicker. *My imagination.* But then she gently lifted some hair to see that bruises were healing. He was starting to look completely white, with fur growing over the 'bald' spots. Not knowing why, she hugged him around his neck, tears forming in her eyes. In such a short time, she felt attached to this ball of fur, but with people, it was so different. She caught a runaway tear with her mitten. "Can you shake hands?"

He lifted a paw and Lexi grabbed it. "I'm going to find a

way to keep you with me wherever I go. Maybe Judy can file a request that we be put in the same foster homes. We can't stay in Smicksburg forever…

"Lexi, what's wrong?"

Lexi gasped. "Ida, I didn't even see you there. Did you hear?"

"*Jah*, some of it. You want to keep the dog and live in Smicksburg is what I gathered."

Straightening up and trying to look nonchalant, she said, "I couldn't think of anything to say to White. He likes the sound of my voice. I made it all up."

Ida put her hands on her hips. "I never want to leave Smicksburg like my *bruder* did."

"You're what?"

"My brother, as you English say. Matthew. He left for the fancy world."

"And you can't visit? Long way by horse and buggy?"

Ida's eyes darkened. "He left the Amish and we don't talk to him."

"Why? Was he bad? Dangerous to be around? Deals drugs?"

Ida cocked her head back. "*Nee*. He broke his promise to the church to be Amish."

"People break promises all the time," Lexi said.

"It's like a marriage vow, very serious," Ida informed. "We depend on each other and can't last as a People if breaking the baptismal vow doesn't have a serious penalty." She bent down and scooped up some snow to form a snowball. "And he lied to God. Broke a promise to God."

"Angela says God loves us and forgives us for anything."

"Matthew won't ask for forgiveness. Doesn't believe in God any more. He says we're all *furhoodled*."

"Fur-what?"

Ida grinned. "*Furhoodled*. It's Pennsylvania Dutch for mixed up in the head." She threw the snowball with gusto and it landed far off into the woods. "My *opa* died shortly after Matthew left. Some think he died of a broken heart."

"What's an *opa*?"

"*Ach*, what you English call grandfather. Matthew and my grandfather were very close."

Ida threw another snowball and Lexi stared at it in the air. "So, you think people acting bad can kill someone?"

Ida shook her head. "Don't know." She threw another snowball. "Sure miss playing baseball. I can hit homeruns and it makes the boys mad. Want to try?"

Lexi handed Ida the leash, let her backpack fall to the ground and threw a snowball, too. "Not nearly as far as yours."

"What's in the bag? Material?"

Lexi groaned. "Homework. I have to find time to do it."

"What subjects?"

"M-A-T-H. I hate it."

"I love it. I can help."

"Really?" Lexi cheered. "Thanks. I was going to ask since you look smart." Her eyes met her new friends and she oddly felt at home with this girl.

~*~

Lexi stepped inside Emma's house while Ida went to the barn to finish her chores. But Lexi stopped in her tracks when she heard crying. "Emma, are you alright?"

"I'll b-be out," Emma said from her kitchen.

Lexi crossed the room to her usual rocker, right next to Emma's. "Sit, White."

The dog's tale flapped like a flag and then sat. "Good boy."

Emma soon appeared from around the corner, a wooden box in her hands. "I'm sorry. This is Atley's tool box and I was reminiscing. Sometimes it seems like he's still in this house."

Lexi froze. "Like his ghost is here?"

"*Nee*. Atley's with the Lord in heaven. 'To be absent in body is to be present with the Lord' the Good Book says. I just mean is seems like he's here." She fondly stroked the cherry stained box. "He was a *gut* carpenter and could carve anything with this here kit." She slowly placed it on the floor. "Enough of my silliness. We live for today, *jah*?"

"You think it's bad to talk about the dead?'

"*Ach, nee*, just about things we can't change. We have to accept all that is put in our lives."

71

Lexi felt indignant all of a sudden. "Am I supposed to just accept my parents are in jail?"

Emma picked up the basket full of cut out hearts and then passed it to Lexi. "Can you change it?"

"No," Lexi blurted.

"Then accept it as God's plan."

"What?"

"Well, be thankful, too. You got out of an abusive home and you live with the Stotlers."

"I'd rather have normal parents. Why should I be thankful for any of it?" White laid his big head on Lexi's feet. *He understands me...*

"I know it's hard to accept. My grandson is shunned and I may never see him again. I can't change it though and so I accept it."

"Emma," Lexi said, appalled. "By accepting it, it seems like you don't care about your grandson."

Emma lifted a hand over her heart. "I never said it wasn't painful. I pray for Matthew daily. I forgive him. He just can't be a part of my life. There's a time, honey, when you have to stop trying to change people."

"Why?"

"Because they don't want to change and God gave us free will, even he won't force them."

"What's free will?" Lexi asked, slouching in her chair.

"Freedom to choose. I'm sure God never wanted your parents to be drug addicts, but that was their choice. Understand?"

What? Lexi always thought she must be cursed by God to have such parents, but maybe it had nothing at all to do with God. *It had everything to do with her parents?* She'd been so angry at church when people talked about God's love.

"What are you thinking?" Emma asked.

Lexi picked up a green checkered heart, needle and thread. "I thought I had bad karma."

"Bad what?"

"Karma. Kids say it. It's when you're jinxed."

Emma clucked her tongue. "I told you it wasn't true. Being jinxed says God isn't fair. That he made some people to have miserable lives and others to have *gut* happy ones. *Nee*, it's the choices people make that form their lives."

"And others," Lexi spouted, flailing her arms in the air.

"Lexi. Hold your temper."

"I can't. My parent's stupid decisions have ruined my life!"

Emma put a hand to Lexi's face. "If you let them…"

"Let them what?" Lexi wanted to turn her face, feeling that Emma was treating her like a baby, but at the same time cherished her genuine concern.

"If you *let* your parents ruin your life." Emma said, gently. "I see other women my age with their husbands and I could be bitter. I see whole families together, no shunned grandson. But I don't *let* it ruin my life, understand?"

"How?" Lexi asked, wanting advice from Emma and fearing it just the same."

She gave a faint smile and then resumed her sewing. "By telling the Lord how I feel when I'm upset and pity myself. He takes my heavy heart and lifts it."

"You tell God you're upset?"

"*Jah*, of course. He knows it anyhow." After making a French knot for the eye of a dove she was embroidering, and set her embroidery hoop down. "Tell God you don't understand and how mad you are."

"I can't," Lexi said, reaching over to pet White.

"Why?"

"Because I'm *really* mad at him."

Emma turned to her. "He knows that, Lexi. Talk to him like a friend."

Friend? This was getting weird. Was Emma that lonely she was talking to God as a friend?

The wooden door opened and in came Ida. "Lexi, I just got washed up. Need help with math?"

"I need to sew hearts first," Lexi said. "You can help."

"Okay. They look great hung up all over town."

"And they're selling," Emma added. "I sold two quilts yesterday, too. Unusual, but I'm thankful." She shifted in her chair. "Lexi, Angela came in and we chatted. She was there when one quilt sold. Nine-hundred dollars. Angela helped convince the customer to buy."

"That's great," Lexi said.

"And we had a little chat about your school. Seems like you need to improve your reading."

Lexi moaned. "I can read fine. It's reading in front of the whole class I hate."

"Why?"

"I get nervous and stutter and can't spit the words out."

Emma handed her little black Bible to Lexi. "I told Angela I'd help by listening to you read. Since Christmas is coming up, how about Luke 2, the Christmas story. Here, you read it in front of Ida and me."

Even though it was cool inside, another log needing to be put in the woodstove, Lexi began to sweat. "Do I have to?"

"I told Angela you would," Emma continued.

Lexi grabbed the Bible and opened it to the passage. "Okay, but no laughing."

"Why would we laugh?" Ida asked.

"Oh, the kids at my school do." She cleared her throat and began to read.

And it came to pass in those days, that there went out a decree from Caesar Augustus, that all the world should be taxed. (Ana this taxing was first made when Cyrenius was governor of Syria.) And all went to be taxed, every one into his own city. And Joseph also went up from Galilee, out of the city of Nazareth, into Judaea, unto the city of David, which is called Bethlehem; (because he was of the house and lineage of David) To be taxed with Mary his espoused wife, being great with child. And so it was, that, while they were there, the days were accomplished that she should be delivered. And she brought forth her firstborn son, and wrapped him in swaddling clothes, and laid him in a manger; because there was no room for them in the inn.

Lexi looked up. "Want me to read more?"

"That was perfect," Ida exclaimed. "Why do kids tease you?"

Lexi shrugged. "I can't read like that in class."

"Why?" Ida asked.

"I don't know. There's twenty-five in the class. It's scary."

"You may just need practice in a small group, then a little bigger, until you can read in public," Emma said.

Lexi knew why she wasn't nervous. Emma and Ida were so kind and she felt right at home among the Amish. Then an idea darted into her mind. *Could she be Amish?*

Chapter 8

The Homeless Man

$\mathcal{A}$ spotlight landed on John and Lexi outside the Methodist Church. "Why aren't we inside with the others?"

"Paint and varnish gives me a headache. And I need to be outside more, right? And it's a clear night." He pointed upwards. "See the Big Dipper?"

Lexi wanted to say she wasn't five years old. Of course she knew what this constellation looked like.

"Come here and help sand while I paint Joseph's hands. Frost bite made them come right off," he said, chuckling at his own joke.

Lexi took the sandpaper and reluctantly began to sand the life-sized wooden Joseph. "Why am I doing this?"

"This set is old and a real pro artist would have to paint it. So, Pastor Dale suggested we make it an all white silhouette. Put a spotlight on it."

"No, I mean why am *I* working on this project. I can be

making money over at Emma's."

Ice crystals jetted out with John's sigh. "Lexi, there's more to Christmas than selling stuff. How about the real meaning?"

"I know it."

Silence filled the crisp air the moon helped illuminate the night.

"Lexi, I wanted to work on Joseph because he's my hero."

"Your hero? A Bible character?" Lexi wanted to laugh but bit her lips together hard.

"Joseph was a foster dad, like me. He wasn't Jesus' real dad, you know."

Lexi had never thought of this. In the Bible, God was Jesus' dad, not Joseph. "And you like being a foster dad?" she dared to ask, knowing the problems she caused.

"I know how it feels to be abandoned," he said slowly. "Raised by my grandparents."

I've never met John's parents, Lexi realized. "I thought your parents were dead."

"They are. Car accident when I was a kid. I actually thought they did it on purpose because I set the woods on fire."

Lexi sat on a stool near John. "You were a bad kid?"

"Sometimes. I let a bonfire get out of control. I was eleven. It spread into the woods and well, the next day their accident happened. I thought they'd rather be dead than have a kid like me."

Images of her dad raging over her spilling a gallon of milk all over the kitchen raced through her mind. She wasn't even in school yet. *You'll put me in an early grave,*" he's screamed, face close to hers. Close enough to slap. She put a hand to her cheek, a phantom pain still lingering.

"So, I was a year younger than you and I thought I killed my parents. It's why Angela and I take in older foster kids. We want them to know that kids will be kids, not perfect." He put a stroke of white paint on Joseph's praying hands.

"Are you going to take in someone else since Tricia left?"

"I don't think so," John said. "My hair's getting blotches of white."

"What? Your hair's dark."

"They're some gray, too."

"Are you giving up being foster parents?" Lexi asked, dread filling her from head to toe.

"No, but as usual, Angela and I take New Years Day and pray and set goals. We ask God to show us what's up for the next year."

"And if God says to give up foster care, will you?"

John eyes met hers. "Lexi, you have nothing to worry about."

"I can stay with you? Forever?"

John turned his head towards the heavens. "I hope so."

Hope? Hope was something that Emma wanted her to

believe in but hope always left her in a dark place. Nothing she'd hoped for ever happened. "Hope so? That means N-O." Lexi stomped a foot. "I knew you wanted to talk to me alone out here. You use varnish in your woodshop. Just tell me."

"That's not true. Doc said to be outside and I get headaches from paint. My woodshop windows are always open and –"

"You don't want me as a foster kid, do you? Is that why Tricia left? You're slowly unloading kids like unwanted pets?"

John stood up, eyes wide. "I'm trying to tell you about my past so you know I understand you. The guilt you carry. And why I'm a foster dad. About my grandparents and all." He put down the Mason jar filled with paint and grabbed Lexi by the shoulders. "You're not leaving our house if I have anything to do with it? Understand? I love you like a daughter."

Tears filled his eyes and Lexi wanted to hug him for the first time, but she felt paralyzed by fear. *Fear in John's eyes.* He was worried about something and it had to do with her staying. He was seeing the doctor more than usual. Was he sick? Too sick to care for kids?

"I, ah, have a headache," she blurted.

"I'm sorry, Lexi. When I talk about my parents I get emotional and at my age, it's a shame. But things stick with you. Did I scare you?"

"It's alright," Lexi forced herself to say.

"Angela said when I finally spill the beans, she gets

headaches, too. I'm a stuffer. I keep things inside and then spill them out like an avalanche."

"It's alright," Lexi repeated. "Can I go home now?"

"By yourself?"

"I'm almost thirteen…" *She wasn't a baby.* Streetlights everywhere and only a few blocks to walk. "I'll be fine."

John nodded reluctantly, and then Lexi spun around and sprinted away. This wasn't the first time she'd run away, a reason why she was still in foster care. She'd almost put her former foster parents in the grave and most likely, she was making John sick.

~*~

Lexi left no note as she and White made a run for it. "Life will be good, White. You can depend on me." Knowing how dark it was when entering farm country, she only grabbed a flashlight.

Darkness cast a long reach over the fields. She noticed the full moon was now half hidden behind clouds. "Let's go boy," she yelled as she picked up the pace.

But White must have mistaken her command and jetted full force ahead, Lexi not able to hold on to the leash. "White!"

The dog darted into Emma's but continued to race out into the back pasture. "Stop!" she yelled.

But he didn't, and she squeezed through the split rail fence and followed him. Sounds of farm animals bellowed and she thought of Emma's bull. "Lord, don't let him gorge me to death," she screamed up at the sky.

Lexi felt mud patches under her feet and then icy earth. But the smell soon told her she was stomping in manure. "*UGH!* White, stop, right now!"

But the dog continued out of the pasture and into unfamiliar woods. Lexi could run no longer. *My lungs will get frost bit*, she thought. *Or I'll die of this smell on me first.*

"White, where are you?" She screamed, her temper flaring. "You come here."

To her shock, White did come to her but nudged her forwards.

"What's wrong with you?" She tried to grab the leash, but he was off again into the woods.

She followed and soon saw a glow coming from a window. We're on another farm already? But as she approached there appeared to be a cabin or an outbuilding for animals. *Someone out milking cows or goats*, she reasoned.

Lexi heard a man's voice. He was talking to White but called him Wolf. *What?* Lexi snuck closer to the window and peeked in. White was lathering up this old mans face. Did he know him? She was always warned to not be friendly with strangers, but she needed to get White. Throwing caution to the frigid wind that was picking up, she stood in the doorway. "That's my dog mister. I need to take him home."

As he raised his head, his wrinkled face had tears running down it like rivulets. "He found me. Looks good."

"Found you? What do you mean?"

"He was my dog."

Lexi heart beat against her ribcage. "You didn't take very good care of him. He's mine now."

He stroked White's fur. "I'm glad."

"Here, White," Lexi commanded. "We're going home."

"I tried," he said. "Not enough food to go around. Tried to pay my taxes but couldn't and here I am, living in an abandoned outbuilding."

Lexi smelt smoke and then finally started to notice the interior of this so-called home. A small fire was burning, made mostly of twigs and what appeared to be lumber. A sleeping bag and cast iron skillet, bags of who know what lined up against one wall. No table, only the chair he was sitting on. Compassion for this man gripped her. He looked so much like Mr. Beech, her elderly neighbor.

"Can I get you some food?"

"I know how to forage," he quickly said, dismissing her.

"Forage? What's that?"

"Hunt for it or find it."

"I don't see any guns…"

"No, I don't hunt anymore, but I set traps. Skin and cook the meat over the fire like when I was a kid." A gleam of light shone in his pale blue eyes. "I always wanted to be Davy Crocket."

"Who's that?"

"Davy Crockett, King of the Wild Frontier? You don't know who that is?"

"A mountain man? Lexi guessed.

"Ya, he was and now so am I. Sick of trying to scrounge around enough money just to live. Now I live off the land."

Lexi was intrigued. *Freedom to live in the woods all the time?* But then she thought of White and how he suffered for this man's so-called freedom. "Your dog didn't get enough to eat off the land."

He hung his head. "Hardest thing I've done. Left him in front of an Amish farm a few miles away. Knew they'd feed him."

"Well, he came crying to my house." Lexi's brows knit together. "Whose land is this?"

"I don't know. Think it's the Schlaubaugh's, but no one comes near here." He rubbed White's back. "He must have smelt the squirrel furs I have mounted outside and found me."

"Well, he's not staying!" Lexi yelled. "He had bruises…"

"When he got scratched up in some barbed wire trying to find food, I knew when I lost the house, I'd be losing him, too. Can't stand to see an animal suffer."

Lexi had to admit she believed him, and since he looked so

much like Mr. Beech, she'd help him. "I'll take White home and get you some stuff. I'll be back tomorrow after supper."

He raised a hand. "My name's Sam. What's yours?"

"Lexi. She gave a faint smile and ran outside and called for White, fear choking her that he'd want to stay with this man. "White," she called again, but he didn't come.

Sam soon appeared in the door, hands on his hips. "I have plenty of food now. He can stay."

"He's mine," Lexi blurted in disbelief.

"Let him decide," Sam said, eyes begging.

Lexi knew White was loyal and he'd be staying with Sam. *I always lose everything*, she thought, biting back tears. She waved good-bye and sulked as she forced one foot in front of another. But her heart was breaking, so she ran with all her might towards Emma's.

When she got out of the woods, a white blob darted past her. She could see through her tears it was White. She knelt down and cried. White licked her face, waiting for a command. Flinging her arms around him, she yelled up to the moon. "Thank you, God. I need White."

~*~

A car pulled up to the house and Lexi heard John and Angela laughing. Laughing, something they rarely did when together with her. She was a burden, she knew. And like John said, he was getting gray in spots, she just hadn't noticed. But she had to postpone running away since she got off to a bad start, not making much ground. And she needed clean clothes…

"Lexi, are you upstairs?" John yelled.

"Yes, in bed. Headache," she lied.

Footsteps mounting the stairs by twos told Lexi John was concerned. "How are you?"

She rubbed her stomach. "My head and stomach hurt and I was afraid…I'd throw up all over the place."

Angela appeared beside John. "You should have let me walk you home."

Angela was a worry-wart to a fault, but it did make Lexi feel like she cared. "Sorry."

John put an arm around Angela. "She said she was nauseated and ran home. Back to see Dr. Adams already."

Angela sped down the hall, soon appearing with a thermometer. "Let me take your temp."

Lexi sucked on the thermometer and then rubbed her tongue on it. Friction, she'd learned in school, creates heat. Rub your hands together and they get warm. She hoped she could get a shocking temperature, one that would put her in isolation at the hospital for months. No school for a month would be heaven.

After the beep, Angela withdrew the thermometer. "It's normal."

John came in and sat on her desk chair. "Lexi, I don't mean to embarrass you, but are you sure there's nothing else wrong?"

"What do you mean?"

"Well, people who spit up sometimes also have…intestinal problems."

Angela gasped. "Diarrhea? Is that what I smell?"

Lexi felt her cheeks warm. "Yes, it's coming from the bathroom."

"I was just in it. No it's not…"

John cocked an eyebrow. "White," he called.

White came out from under Lexi's bed, tail between his legs.

Angela yelled, "You reek. You reek of…"

John rolled his eyes. "Manure."

"Lexi," Angela muttered, "what's this about."

John took White by the collar to lead him to his bath. Angela crossed her arms, hurt emanating from her pretty eyes. "You promised to stop lying."

"I didn't. White went wild when we left for home and pulled me. He practically dragged me through Emma's fields and then into the next farm over. We got manure all over us."

"You said you had diarrhea."

"Oh, I did, after the whole thing. The smell of manure turned my stomach."

"Really?" Angela mocked. "But you're fine here in bed with

that same smell right under your nose. Lexi, why tell lies?"

"I don't. When we got back, first I got sick in the stomach but then I got a runny nose. I can't smell a thing now."

Angela darted up and paced the floor. "I need to call Judy. Maybe your case manager can get some straight answers from you." She held onto the back of the desk chair. "Lexi, aren't you happy here?"

"What?"

"I need an honest answer. It's important."

"I don't want to go to another foster home," Lexi blurted. "Please, let me stay here."

Angela face softened as if relieved. "Are you really sure?"

"Yes," Lexi panicked. "Don't send me away."

"Well, Judy's coming tomorrow after school for another in-home visit. Lots to talk about." Shoulders slumped, she said, "I'm tired. We'll talk tomorrow."

Lexi's said good-night and turned over so Angela couldn't see her chin quivering. She was such a baby to cry at her age, but she let the tears flow. Angela was so good to her and she was killing her with worry.

Chapter 9

Saving Emma's Quilt Shop

Emma pressed her kerosene iron against the wrinkled gingham material by the glow of the oil lamp. "Green", she pined. "Atley's favorite color." Memories of them decorating their house with pines invaded her mind and soon she felt that wave of grief threaten to overtake her. *My first Christmas without my beloved. My first Christmas without Matthew, my dear grandson. Lord, it's too hard.*

But a slice of hope filled Emma. Through the Amish grapevine, she'd heard that Matthew was in Homer City, an hour away, and was living with Old Order Mennonites. *Better than the fancy world*, she supposed.

"Emma, are you here?"

"In my bedroom," Emma informed, glad to have Lexi here as a distraction. Still staring at the green heart, she asked the Lord for strength. Lexi shuffled slowly into the room, White by her side, Emma knew right then how to overcome her holiday depression: by reaching out more to Lexi and others in need. Blessed are those who give, and Lexi had been crying.

Lexi ran to her and hugged her around the middle. "I want to be Amish," she blurted. "They keep promises."

"What do you mean?"

"Ida said to break a promise is serious. You get shunned for it."

"*Jah*," Emma said, pulling Lexi tight and smoothing her disheveled brown hair. "What's this have to do with Lexi Remington?"

"The caseworker came and asked me lots of questions."

"And?"

"She asked Angela and John, too."

"And?"

"This always happens when foster parents can't take it anymore."

Emma knew Lexi had been in five other foster homes before coming to Smicksburg. She was also aware of what was going on over at Angela's, but it might frighten Lexi. And it was confidential. "Lexi, I don't think you'll be leaving the Stotlers anytime soon."

Lexi pulled away and ogled at Emma. "You know something, don't you?"

Not wanting to lie, Emma slowly sat down in her rocker, pondering what to say. "Time, Lexi. God makes all things beautiful in His time."

"Well, God lost my clock or something. Nothing's right or

on time," Lexi snapped, flinging herself onto the bed.

"Lexi, do you trust me?" Emma prodded, sitting next to her, rubbing her back.

She was laying face down, but Emma saw her head bob up and down.

"Okay, then. You be the best girl you can over at Angela's and wait."

"Wait for what?"

"Christmas."

"Christmas? Why?"

"There's going to be a change you'll like."

"I can be Amish?" Lexi sprang up from the bed.

Cold air flew into the room and loud stomping came from the living room. Emma cocked an eyebrow. "They're here."

"Who?"

"Your audience. You're afraid to read in front of your class, so you're going to practice in front of my *grandkinner* and some of their friends. Ida arranged it."

"No," Lexi said evenly. "I can't."

"Ida's been helping you with math and doing a *gut* job. Now she wants to help with reading. She really cares about you."

A smile slid across Lexi's face. "Wish Ida was my sister."

Emma gripped Lexi's shoulder. "She feels the same way."

"Really? For real? I mean, like a real sister?" Lexi blurted in a rapid string.

Emma snickered. "*Jah.* Now, let's go read." Exiting her bedroom, Emma's heart warmed as Ida embraced Lexi and introduced her to many cousins and friend, twenty in all, squished into the living room.

Ida gave Lexi her grandma's Bible as she took White by the collar. "Start at Luke 2:8" passage" where you left off, "she said", and then Ida led White to sit on the floor by her.

Lexi looked like a deer in headlights at the group and then began to read.

And there were in the same c-c-county.

"Country," Ida said softly.

Lexi nodded as her face instantly turned red.

And there were in the same country sheferds..."

"Shepherds," Ida said, getting up to stand by Lexi, the dog by her side.

Lexi glanced around, her face pinched. "Sorry…

"*And there were in the same country shepherds abiding in the f-field, keeping watch over their flock by night.*

And, lo, the angel of the Lord came upon them, and the glory of the Lord sh-shone r-round about them: and they were sore afraid.

And the angel said unto them, F-Fear not: for, behold, I bring you good tidings of great joy, which shall be to all people.

For unto you is born this day in the city of D-David a S-Savior, which is Christ the Lord."

Lexi meekly looked up to clapped hands.

"*Gut* job when Ida's standing by ya," Benny said.

Emma saw right away what Lexi's problem was. It wasn't reading at all, it was having lots of eyes on her. Lexi also carried so much shame, but her slumped shoulders became more erect as Ida stood beside her. "Okay, kinner, outside you go."

"Can't we stay for hot chocolate," Benny asked. "I smell it."

Emma threw her hands up. "All of you? Not enough." She leaned down and scooted Benny out of her house. "Bye, *kinner*. *Danki* for listening." She clasped her hands and turned to Lexi. "You did *gut* when Ida was up there with you. You don't like being the center of attention, *jah*?"

"Usually w-when I'm in the center of attention I'm in t-trouble," Lexi fumbled for words. "When the teacher yells, or my dad yelled in front of people."

Emma bit her lower lip. Had her father humiliated her in public that she was so frightened to read at school? *Lord help this girl that's captured my heart.*

The door opened again and Emma turned to say, "Benny, I said –"

"It's me, Angela. Came to work on hearts."

"*Ach*, come on in. Benny's a rascal," Emma mused.

Angela threw off her coat and hung it on a peg near the door. "I could live in this tiny house. So little to clean." When her eyes met White's she took a step back. "Keep him there!"

Ida laughed. "He's not going to hurt you."

"He could rip my leg off, he's so huge."

Emma told Ida to take White into her bedroom and then lifted the basket of pre-cut hearts up to Angela. "Take your pick."

Angela chose a red calico. "That dog's driving me nuts."

"He's been good," Lexi stated firmly.

"I know, but I'm still afraid." Angela sat down in a cozy rocker. "So, Emma, how many hearts have you sold?"

"Not enough," Emma said. "I don't think the signs leading to my shop are big enough."

"John can fix that. And how about advertising?"

"In the English papers? It's a fortune."

"I know," Angela said. "But the internet would have people swarming your shop, like I told you."

"*Jah*, but we Amish can't use it."

"I can," Angela said slowly, as if deep in thought. "I think it would double the business."

"If we double the business, I wouldn't have enough to sell. Need more hands…" Emma knew Angela desperately wanted to work from home. She was a skilled sewer and made crafts of all kinds. "How's are things at the Smicksburg Library, Angela?"

"I'd like more hours. Only twenty a week and I fear it may close. Seems like the world's gone digital, and there's no need for books anymore."

"No books?" Ida asked. "How can that be?"

"Well, are books in the library, but then lots of electronic readers that the kids use, but most have them at home, so the library's pretty dead. Doing *another* fund-raiser to keep it open…"

Emma leaned forward. "Do you like your job?"

"It takes care of a few bills…."

"If we had more business in the store with the internet, I'd need help…."

Angela put her calico heart down. "Are you offering me a job?"

Emma grinned. "You'd have to get that net thing to work and bring in customers, but, *jah*, why not try it."

"Net thing?" Angela asked.

"The internet," Lexi quipped. "Angela, you'd be so good at this. You could walk to work and do crafts all day."

Angela beamed. "How exciting."

Emma could spend time with Angela 'til the cows came home. Atley would want her to move on. "Expand your shop," he'd said. No one could fill Atley's shoes but she needed to move forward. Was this her Lord prompting her?

~*~

95

Lexi promised Angela she'd avoid any cow pastures when taking White for a walk while she chatted with Emma about the possibility of being partners in business. But Lexi had a mission to accomplish. Get food to Sam.

She pondered Emma's words as she marched through the snow. Emma didn't say she couldn't be Amish, but that there was change coming and not to worry. But all Lexi heard was *change, change, change*. Fear crept up her back like an icy grip. "Come on, White, let's *go*," Lexi said, pulling the dog, hesitant to walk any further. "Are you so big and old you can't keep up?"

White put his nose in the air and took the lead, Lexi trailing him. "Not through the pasture," she screamed.

White turned, and cocked one furry ear.

"You understand? Good boy. Now, let's go to Sam's."

White sprang forward again, Lexi running, her knuckles white on the leash. "White, I didn't say go like a crazy dog."

The dog ran faster until they were near the old abandoned out building where Sam lived. As she raised a hand to knock on the wooden door, it opened. "Davy Crockett here. This is Indian Territory," he said firmly. "Do you have permission to pass?"

Lexi stared at his coon-tailed cap, and then grinned. "It's me, Lexi. Your dog's here to see you."

"What dog? I don't have a dog, only a horse."

Lexi pulled White near her. "This dog was yours, remember? And there's no horse here," she said looking outside.

"He's riding with Cornplanter."

"Who's that?"

"An Indian chief."

Lexi wondered when Sam would stop joking. "Can we come in, it's cold out here." She turned so he could see her backpack. "Snuck some food for you."

He put a hand up in protest. "I live off the land."

Lexi smirked. "Hot biscuits and a jar or honey…"

"Well, I do need bread and can't find any bees this time of year. Come in."

Lexi noticed upon entering the building that it wasn't much warmer than outside, and it looked messy. "Where's your fire?"

"Over there," he said, pointing to old burnt out logs.

"Well, you let it go out but I can fire it up." Lexi let White go but he stayed near her as she took some of the candy bar wrappers and old newspapers lying in a corner. She threw them on the logs and began to blow. A spark and then a yellow glow appeared and she lit a piece of paper, stuffing it in, and soon there was a small fire. "Now, that'll be better."

"Thank you, Margaret," Sam said.

"I'm Lexi. Don't you remember?"

He stared right through her. "Do you want me to play you something on my harmonica? Still have the knack."

Lexi nodded and he pulled out his instrument from the pocket of his worn out jeans. He placed it to his lips and an awful song came out, something he must have just made up. Lexi wanted to put her fingers in her ears and even White seemed to be in pain, whining as the song continued. He looked thinner, his cheek bones sticking out, making his face creepy. *Should she tell Angela and John about Sam? Maybe he needs help.* Lexi squirmed. No, she hoped to be Amish so keeping a promise was something she needed to get better at.

He took a break, apparently out of breath. He coughed, leaning over, his body shaking.

"Sam, do you need any medicine? I can get it…"

He eyed her. "Davy Crockett doesn't need medicine."

Was he joking? If he was, he was taking it too far.

"Margaret, now it's your turn."

Margaret? She was Lexi, but she didn't want to keep correcting him. "My turn for what?"

"Oh, you always made me plead. Sing me a song."

Lexi, feeling more confused than ever, but wanting to cheer up Sam, had only one song on her mind, the one Angela picked for the children's choir to sing on Light-Up-Night. "Okay, I'll sing."

Love came down at Christmas,
Love all lovely, Love Divine,
Love was born at Christmas,

Stars and Angels gave the sign.

Lexi stopped. Sam was crying. "What's wrong?"

He swatted the tears away. "My mama sang that."

"And it makes you sad that she's…dead?"

"Dead? My mama's dead?" he asked, fear tightening his face.

"Well, I don't know. You're old. I just figured."

"I'm not old." Sam got up and headed towards Lexi. "I'm only sixteen."

White lowered his ears and stood in front of Lexi.

Feeling sorry for Sam, yet now fearful, Lexi picked up White's leash. "We best get going." Sliding off her backpack, she quickly withdrew the bag of biscuits and tossed them to Sam. "I'll put the jar of honey right here on the ground –"

"I'm sorry. Did I scare you?"

"No. Not at all. I just need to get going."

"Will you visit again?" Sam asked, eyes drooping.

Lexi felt for this old man. "Sure. Real soon."

"Bye, Margaret…"

Chapter 10

A Gift?

Lexi was relieved it was Friday, little homework except to finish reading *A Christmas Carol* and math. And then only a week until Christmas break. She wanted to jump, skip and twirl all at the same time at the idea, but only free-fell on her bed and relished the thought of *two weeks out of jail!* Mr. Allison, her science teacher, overheard her calling Winter Break, Out of Jail Break and he tried to make her feel guilty. *Some kids don't get to go to school in poor countries,* he'd said, but it didn't work. She loved to learn, but had her eye on a one-room schoolhouse when she got became Amish. When Ida told her she was going to try to convince her parents to adopt her, hope rose within.

She heard Angela call her from downstairs and she ran out in the hallway, wanting to ride the banister down again, but showed self-control.

As she entered the kitchen, she saw Angela and John at the table, both avoiding eye contact with her. A pain darted into her stomach. *She was leaving. Judy found her a new place.* She'd worn out Angela and John completely.

"Lexi, sit down," John said, rapidly twiddling his thumbs. "We need to talk."

Lexi felt like a sheep going before the shearers: terrified. She slunk into her regular spot at the table. "What's the matter?"

Angela cleared her throat. "Miss Robin called. She said you've been cheating."

Lexi gasped. "Is that all?"

"Is that all?" Angela said, raising her voice. "Lexi, we've worked hard on telling the truth."

"I thought since Judy was here, I was leaving. I'm not, am I?"

John's mellow eyes met hers. "Not today. But why did you cheat?"

"I didn't. When I go to Emma's, Ida teaches me math."

"She *does* your math. Miss Robin said not only has your homework been flawless, but it's not in your handwriting…number writing," Angela crowed.

"She does it with me. I understand it all better when I talk about it. She writes the problem down and then makes up a story so I understand it, and when I get it, she writes it all down."

John tapped Lexi's shoulder. "You're telling the truth, aren't you?"

Lexi noticed an odd emotion well up inside of her. It felt good to tell the truth. And she'd worked so hard at math, it made her feel smart. "I am telling the truth."

Angela leaned on an elbow. "Can you do a problem for us?"

Angela didn't believe her. She clenched her jaw shut, wanting to yell that she no longer lied, but simply nodded.

John wrote a few numbers on a piece of paper and slid it in front of her.

-10 + - 49 + - 45 = _____

Lexi stared at the problem, not remembering a thing Ida told her about negative numbers. She glanced at John and then Angela, eyes round. "My mind's blank."

Angela bit her fingernails. "What would Ida tell you to do?"

What would Ida tell her? She needed her here right now. She looked at the problem, but negative numbers freaked her out. What had Ida said? A picture of a thermometer came to her. She sucked in air, not realizing she wasn't breathing, and then raised both hands and yelled "Yes! I remember."

Go on then and do the problem," Angela said, relief in her voice.

"Well, if it's 10 below zero, and then it goes 49 degrees lower that's 59 below. Then if it goes down 45 degrees, it's 104 degrees below zero, so the answer is -104."

John threw his hands up, too. "Yes! That's right."

"Ida helped you by using a thermometer?" Angela asked, amazed.

"Yes. I was petrified to see a negative number because I'd

never seen one, but Ida said I see them all the time."

"So you didn't understand until you could apply it," Angela said slowly.

"Ida's math book is full of word problems and they're fun. It's why I want to go to Amish school."

"You're not Amish," John said. "And foster kids have to go to public school."

"Jail," Lexi said under her breath.

"Jail?" Angela said, leaning towards her. "It's that bad? Lots of kids go…"

"I don't like how big the classrooms are or being the center of attention. Emma had me read in front of lots of her grandkids and I started to stutter, all nervous. Ida stood by me, along with White, and I could read, just like that."

"So you'd do better in a smaller classroom? Angela prodded. "Or be tutored?"

John drummed his fingers on the table. "Let me talk to your mom about this."

Lexi let our nervous laughter. "My mom? What's she have to do with this?"

"Oh, I'm sorry. Slip of the tongue," John said. "I mean Angela."

Angela took his hand from across the table. "John and I had many talks with our girls at this table. We always talked later about it in private."

"Ali and Elyse cheated in school?" Lexi asked.

"Oh, ya," John said with a chuckle. "Now, that's probably popped out a few gray hairs."

Laughter echoed around the room, Lexi included. *Ali and Elyse weren't perfect. Maybe she was just a normal sixth grader after all. Maybe she wasn't putting John and Angela in the grave.*

~*~

That night at Emma's, the scent of chocolate permeated the tiny room. Lexi dug her socked toes into White's fur as she sewed yet another heart. "Emma, can I go to Amish school even if I'm not Amish...yet?"

"Yet?"

"Ida and I talk about it all the time and she said her dad could teach me all I need to know for baptism."

Emma took a sip of hot chocolate. "He could, if you were old enough to understand."

"What?"

"Lexi, *kinner* don't get baptized until their teenagers. Anyhow, it's hard for someone like you who's always lived fancy to be Amish."

"Fancy? I'm not fancy," Lexi informed. "I'm anything but. Grew up poor, second hand rag clothes to wear. I like Ida's clothes."

"By fancy I mean with electricity and indoor plumbing. Some adults do convert, and make it, but you're a child."

Lexi wanted to scream she was twelve not five! But she started to count mentally to ten and take deep breaths, like Angela taught her. "I'll be a teenager next year."

Emma stood and went into the kitchen. "Want more hot chocolate?"

"No thank you."

When Emma returned, she had a wooden box. "What are you giving John and Angela for Christmas?"

"Making them these hearts I suppose. Don't have much money."

"What if I gave you a percentage of the sales of the hearts and you could earn this tool set?" She took her seat and ran her hand over the wooden box. "Angela and I have been talking about our new business ideas. John can carve and I can sell his items in the store."

"Why doesn't Angela buy it?"

"It would help John realize that you like him," Emma said tenderly.

"He thinks I don't?" Lexi asked. "And he cares that I don't like him?"

"You really don't like him?" Emma asked.

"I never said that. I…well…have a harder time liking men. But I guess I'm starting to like John a lot more." She dug her toes deeper into White, feeling his heartbeat. "John's been talking to me a lot more." Lexi stared at the tool box. "Why are you getting rid of it? It's Atley's."

Emma's eyes misted so she turned her head to work on the red calico heart. "Atley and Matthew used it together before the shunning. Reminds me of my loss too much."

Lexi reached for Emma's hand. "Maybe God brought me here for you to keep you company. I love you Emma."

A tear ran down Emma's cheek and she took Lexi's hand. "And I love you. You're a gift." She pulled a handkerchief out of her apron pocket and wiped her tears. "Matthew's name means 'gift from God' and I'll never understand it all, but the Lord gives and takes, away, blessed be His name."

Emma called her a gift. Emma said she loved her. Maybe she'd be taking Matthew's place? Emma of course was too old to adopt her, but Ida's parents could. She sat continued to work on her red heart and shot an earnest prayer up to heaven. *Please, Lord, make me a part of this family for Christmas.*

"So, Lexi, do you want to earn this box for John?"

Lexi nodded. John would know she appreciated how he gained her trust. Him only being down the street when she became Amish, she could visit all the time.

White stood erect, ears up and growled. Lexi pat his back. "What is it, boy?"

The dog rushed to the door and started to scratch frantically.

"White," Emma called. "Now stop it. You'll scrape the

varnish off the door. Come here."

But White didn't stop and Lexi ran to him. "I think he needs to go to the bathroom real bad." She opened the door and a cat was scratching from the other side. White leapt for the cat and a chase ensued. "White, get back here!" Lexi screamed, shoving her boots on.

Emma took her woolen black cape and draped in on her. "Come right back. It's supposed to snow."

The dog ran toward the barn out back, right on the heels of the cat., and Lexi struggled to keep up. But then the cat darted towards Emma's again, so they all encircled the house.

"Lexi," Emma yelled from the porch. "A storm's coming in."

"I can't leave White out here," Lexi shouted back. White ran towards the barn again and then into the back pasture. Lexi pounded her feet into the snow. "Emma, I have to get him. He might get lost and never find home."

"*Nee*, Lexi, come here."

"Sorry, Emma. I have to go."

Chapter 11

~~~

The Snowstorm

$\mathcal{A}$ngela and John paced the floor of Emma's little house. "I'm calling the police," John said. "It's midnight and look at this snow!"

"Three feet," Angela said faintly. "She could be…"

John took Angela by the shoulders. "Honey, don't think like that."

Emma's stomach was in a knot. This was her fault. Lexi had permission to stay until eleven since it was Friday. But she was too afraid of this massive snowstorm that she didn't go for help. "I'm so sorry. I should have gone over to Levi's sooner."

"Emma, then we'd be looking for you. You can't see a foot in front of you in this whiteout," Angela said, giving Emma a hug. "You went over as soon as you could."

"Lots of Amish and English out looking for her," Emma said, her voice shaky.

"I need to get back out there," John snapped. "But I'm calling the police." He pulled his cell phone out as he pulled the front door open, letting in a heap of snow."

"I'm coming, too," Angela said, running after him.

Emma sat in her chair, emptiness enveloping her. *Lord, this is awful. Please guide someone to Lexi. Help all the friends in this little town who are out there…*

~*~

Lexi panicked. She was suffocating. The weight of White on her kept her warm, but she needed air. "White, move. This dugout's too small."

The dog turned and licked her face, and then put his paw on her hand.

"I love you, White," she said. "But move over."

Wind whipped into the dugout she'd made when the storm started to hit. And then more snow. Would she be cocooned in here? "Help!" she yelled once again.

An owl hooted from a nearby tree and then Lexi heard music. Was she dying? Was it the sound of angels? She shook her head. "Angels don't play the harmonica." She hugged White. "We're near Sam's house. White, move out."

The dog jumped out of the piling snow and Lexi held on tight to his leash. "Go to Sam's" she commanded, teeth chattering.

Lexi could only see pure white. "Help me, God," she yelled. "I'm too young to freeze to death."

The sound of the harmonica came a little closer and then she could hear the tune. "Go, White."

The dog sprang ahead and Lexi held on to the leash with all her might. But her fingers were numb and she soon could hold on no longer. But she didn't have to. Someone was holding her hand, leading her forward.

~*~

Lexi opened her eyes to see John and Angela hovering over her. "What happened?"

"Stay awake," John said. "You need to stay awake."

Lexi forced her heavy lids to open, but it seemed impossible. John shook her. "Lexi. Please, stay awake."

Lexi opened her eyes to see a fire burning. "We have a fireplace?"

"No, honey. We're at someone's house."

"You're at Davy Crockett's house," Sam informed, standing erect. "And you're trespassing on Indian Territory."

"I know," John said. "But we'll be gone soon."

A wrapping on the door and someone yelling, and Sam opened the door briskly. "You're on Indian Territory. Retreat!"

Lexi could see two Amish men, rubbing their hands. "Sam, let them in. It's freezing out there."

"You know this man?" John asked Lexi.

She nodded and then her lids weighed down and she gave in to sleep.

"Lexi," Angela cried. "Stay awake. You're half frozen."

Lexi raised one eye. "Okay."

John scooped her up and ran out to the Amish sleigh that was right outside. "Santa?" Lexi asked, staring at the man with the long gray beard.

"My name's Crist and this is my son, Amos."

All Lexi heard was 'Crist' and although she was frozen, her heart began to warm. "Kris Kringle?"

"Nee, Crist Weaver," he said with a chuckle. Soon Angela and John joined in, but Amos looked baffled.

John yelled out into the cold night air. "On Dasher, on Dancer, Prancer and Vixen."

Amos turned around, bewilderment etched into his face.

White jumped into the sleigh, and when other Amish men came along, they stayed with Sam, who kept yelling at them to stay off Indian Territory.

~*~

Lexi opened her eyes and looked down at her hand. A needle was in it. "I hate needles!" she screamed.

"I'm right here, honey. You're in the hospital," Angela calmed her. She placed a cool hand on Lexi's forehead. "You fever went down I think. I hope."

"What's going on? Why am I in here?"

"You're being treated for frostbite. Thanks to White, you'll be fine. That dog saved your life and now I have to admit something."

"What?"

"I love that dog," Angela said, hand clenching her heart.

Memories of White chasing a cat and then seeing Sam. "I'm tired and feel like its hard to think."

"You've been through a lot. The whole town was out looking for you, do you know that?"

"The whole town?"

"Yes, all for Lexi Remington. See, you've very loved in Smicksburg."

"Angela," she said hesitantly, "did I see Santa Claus?"

"It was Old Crist. With his sleigh, you thought he was Santa."

"I remember that. Did you see anyone else?"

"Well, there's a man who's in this hospital, too. He thought he was Davy Crockett."

"Sam? How'd you find him?"

"You know him?" Angela prodded. "Don't tell me you were visiting him."

"I broke my promise. I can't be Amish too good."

Angela took Lexi's hand. "That man's name is Sam, and he's malnourished…"

Lexi looked away. "I took him food."

"What?"

"He was White's owner. He said he had to give White up. White was starving."

Angela shook her head in disbelief. "Well, we brought him

here and it appears that he lost his home. Couldn't pay taxes and he wanted to live off the grid. They said he had a bruise on his head and must have had a concussion, so didn't remember to eat, and got confused."

"He thought her really was Davy Crockett?" Lexi asked.

"Yes. He's on the road to recovery, though. To think there's a homeless man in Smicksburg."

"Poor Sam," Lexi gasped. "We need to take him in."

Angela flashed a gleaming smile. "The church is going to help, along with the Amish. Isn't that something? So much love in our little town."

"That's great," Lexi exclaimed. "Can I see him?"

Angela looked at her watch. "Judy will be here soon."

"Why?"

"Well, she wants to know if you ran away. Did you?"

Lexi tried to sit up but couldn't. "No. White was chasing a cat into the woods and –"

"Lexi, were you going to try to live like 'Davy Crockett'? Tell the truth."

"Well," Lexi said, "Maybe, until I decided I want to be Amish."

"Amish? You're serious about that?"

"Yes. Ida's trying to talk her parents into it…"

Angela bit her lower lip. "You're not happy with us?"

"Yes, but it's foster care, not a real home. If the Amish

promise to take me, they can't give me up. They have to keep their word."

"And you think you could be Amish? Seriously? No jeans, but dresses all the time? Never go out to see a movie –"

"I don't care about all those fancy things. I just want a home."

Judy walked in. "Amish? Lexi Remington, aren't you happy with John and Angela Stotler?"

Lexi's eyes bugged out. "Yes. I don't want to be moved. I didn't run away but just chased after my dog."

Judy put a hand up. "Lexi, slow down." She took a stray chair and plunked herself in it. "Lexi, I know you want to be adopted." She glanced over at Angela. "I also overheard your conversation. To be honest, I was spying, and I like what I see."

Angela's smile split her face, but Lexi didn't know why. Maybe she wasn't going to give up foster care after all. Was it her imagination that there was a secret in the house she knew nothing about? Well, if she could stay until… "Judy, can someone who's in there seventies adopt me? I think someone wants to."

"Who?" Angela gasped.

"Emma. She said I was a gift. She loves me. She's lonely, too, since her husband died. Can she?"

Judy's jaw dropped. "Lexi, you just told me you were happy

with Angela and John."

Lexi wanted to scream, and this time she let it out. "I'm not adopted by them. I want real parents!"

Chapter 12

Joseph was Jesus' foster dad?

Lexi opened her eyes and in the dark, she made out a man staring down at her. "Who are you?" she shouted.

"Lexi, it's John. Waiting for you to wake up."

She looked around to see she was not in her room, but in the hospital. "Why am I here?"

"They'll release you tomorrow. You had mild hyperthermia."

"White saved my life. Did you know that?"

"Yes. And Angela wants to keep him now." He raised a hand and Lexi gave him a high five. "Good job, Lex."

Lex? He'd never called her Lex. But he said it with an emotion she believed was love.

"I got Joseph all done. He looks pretty good." He crossed his legs and arms. "You know, I've been thinking about Joseph quite a bit. He didn't want to marry Mary when he found out it wasn't his kid."

"Really?"

"It's all in the Bible. But God gave Joseph love for Mary and her child. So, Joseph decided to raise him as his own. Imagine God allowing an adoptive parent to raise his son. Pretty trusting, wouldn't you say?"

"Yes."

"And Joseph protected the baby Jesus like he was his own. They had to flee into Egypt and live there two years. All because they had this kid to take care of."

Lexi wondered why John was going on about Joseph, but pretended to be really interested.

"Joseph taught Jesus a trade, too. Being a carpenter in those days, you needed to be homeschooled, I suppose, and Joseph taught Jesus all he knew to make a living."

Lexi turned towards him. "I always wondered why Jesus worked at all. Why not just snap his fingers and make food?"

"He wanted to understand us, so he became a human."

Lexi pulled the blanket up to her chin. Jesus was never a foster kid. How could he understand her?

John riffled thought the pages of his pocket Bible and as he reached up to hit the reading light above the bed.

"This means a lot to me:

He was despised and rejected by mankind, a man of suffering, and familiar with pain. Like one from whom people hide their faces he was despised, and we held him in low esteem.

Despised? Rejected? She'd always thought her dad despised her. She was his big accident. "Why was Jesus despised and rejected if his dad loved him?"

"Well, he was raised poor in Nazareth. People made fun that he came from there. They asked, 'Can anything good come out of Nazareth?' And people didn't understand his message. I mean, he said to love your enemies. That's hard."

"Sure is. I can't stand Rachael at school. She walks around like she's better since she's rich. Makes fun of me. Doesn't believe my...parents are living in Europe."

"Europe? You told kids that at school?"

"What else am I supposed to say? My parents are in jail?"

John leaned towards her. "I guess that would be…"

"Embarrassing."

"No need to be. Lex, can I tell you something. A secret?"

"Okay."

"Well, I found you easier to love than Ali . She was driving Angela and me crazy. What a mouth she had. And temper…." He bellowed out a long whistle. "I found her hard to love."

Lexi frowned. "Really?"

"Yes, but I love her now. God gave me back my love for her. The strength to forgive and move on. You see, Lexi, love originates with God. He keeps things all together. He keeps a family together…"

Confusion filled her. Why was he saying all this? She had no family and probably never would. She turned over. "I'm tired."

"You rest, then. See you tomorrow."

When John walked out of the room, she took the stuffed bear that Pastor Dale brought her and wrung its neck. *Ali and Elyse have such a good dad.* Jealousy overtook Lexi and she realized how awesome it would be to have a dad like John.

~*~

Lexi spun around and eyed Ali and Elyse, home from Christmas vacation, and wanting to take her shopping in Pittsburgh? *Why?* Elyse's earnest eyes frightened her. Was this their way of saying good-bye? Some new clothes since she'd be leaving. Well, she didn't need anything. She'd be Amish. Ida told her she could take the place of her brother who they still set the table for even though shunned.

"I don't want to go to Pittsburgh."

"Why?" Elyse asked, eyes round. "Come on. All girls like to shop."

Lexi raised an eyebrow. "For what?"

"Clothes, shoes, food. It'll be our girls' day out. Ali and I always do it, and this year, you're invited."

Lexi flopped herself on the living room sofa. White was soon leaning his head on her feet. "I don't need clothes."

Ali bent over and felt her head. "Are you sick or something? All girls like to shop for clothes."

Lexi lowered her gaze. "Only fancy girls. I'm plain."

"Oh, honey, you are not. You're really pretty," Ali said, taking a seat next to her. "You're too hard on yourself."

Lexi scooted further away from Ali . "I mean that I'm going to dress plain. Be Amish."

Crossing her arms, Ali stifled a giggle. "I went through that phase. I was your age and didn't want to go to school past eighth grade. Being Amish was in my mind, my ticket out."

"It's not that," Lexi said. "It's to have a home. You don't understand that…"

"Kiddo, I know I don't. But Amish? Seriously?" She stood and tried to pull Lexi up. "We're going shopping for some…boots. Elyse, don't you think she'd look great in ankle boots?"

"Yes I do."

Lexi shrugged her shoulders. "I might need them. Amish wear black boots."

Ali cocked an eyebrow. "Nice ankle boots and a new pair of jeans? Maybe a few new tops?"

Lexi tried to pull away, but Ali held her hands tight. "I'll be wearing an Amish dress and apron. No, I don't need anything."

Ali released Lexi and scrunched up her face. "Does mom know about this?"

"Yes," Lexi said. "Judy, too."

"And they have an Amish family that's going to adopt you?"

Elyse asked.

Lexi nodded. "Emma's daughter Marie and her husband Levi."

"That's weird," Ali said, her voice shaky.

"Why is it weird?"

"I'm surprised. Don't know what to say. Mom didn't tell me." She sat next to Lexi again. "I'll miss you, Kiddo. More attached to you than Tricia."

"I'll be up the road…" Lexi dared to look into Ali 's eyes. They drooped. Ali wasn't a crier, but when sad, her whole face fell.

Angela hummed Jingle Bells as she came into the room. "So, are you girls out for the day?"

Ali shook her head. "No. Lexi doesn't want to go because she's turning Amish? Mom, please fill in the blanks."

Angela stepped back as if dizzy. "There are no blanks. Lexi, no one said you were leaving this house."

Lexi pursed her lips, not knowing how to break this news. "Matthew Yoder was shunned and Ida said I could take his place."

Angela collapsed in the recliner. "What?"

"You know how close Ida and I are now. She thinks God sent me to take her brother's place."

"And what does Marie and Levi say?" Angela blurted.

"Oh, Ida's working on them. You know how smart she is.

It'll take time but they'll be my family." She slowly closed her eyes. "And Emma will be my grandma…"

Angela's pale blue eyes seemed darker. "You're not happy here?"

"Oh, I am, but like I told John, I want a real family. A permanent family."

Angela stared straight ahead as if in a trance. "Lexi, get ready. You're going shopping."

"Do I have to?"

"Yes," Angela said evenly. "You have a family right here. Stop this nonsense about being Amish."

Lexi squinted, trying to think of what to say. Didn't Angela know she was smarter than she looked? All signs pointed to her being moved to another foster home again. It started with the parents getting frustrated with her, and then in *secret* plans were made to get rid of her.

But she had hope. The Amish kept their word. Ida would get her to be a family member. She'd be Lexi Yoder.

~*~

Elyse slid her arm thought Lexi's. "Let's go to Macy's first."

"Ya," Ali quipped. "They have lots of boots for Lexi."

Lexi went through the motions of being excited to shop only because the talk in the car made Elyse and Ali so sad. They wanted her to stay, but had no control over the foster care system.

As they meandered through the crowded mall, huge snowflakes hung from the vaulted ceiling and lights sparkled everywhere. *How magical*, Lexi thought. Up ahead was a train carrying children around a winter wonderland, their parents waved as they came around, phones up, taking pictures. The hole in her heart, feelings of abandonment, shattered the enchantment. *No one's had it harder than me! Why God?*

She tagged along as Elyse and Ali looked in windows, and feelings of rejection flooded her soul. *Jesus, if you felt rejected, can you help me. If you really know how I feel, can you just take away this hurt? I need a place to stay. You had a family. Can you give me one, too?*

She felt somehow like her heart was lighter. Maybe talking to Jesus had the same effect of journaling, getting your feelings out. *Jesus*, she continued, *I hate my parents. They're cruel. If I have to go back there, or to another home, I'm going to live like Sam. I'll hide out in an abandoned building and live off the land. So, if you're real, and you can hear me saying this in my head, I want you to know that I'll run away again. I'm good at it.*

She felt her banging heart ease up. Letting her honest feelings out was good for her. Like Emma told her, 'Tell God how you're feeling. He knows about it anyhow.' *Jesus, I have no more to say to you right now, except this big secret that's being kept from me is driving me nuts. Emma said I had a surprise on Christmas. Angela and John, well, the whole Stotler family is acting weird. So, this surprise might be that someone wants to adopt me, my parents are finally considered unfit, and I'd never see everyone in Smicksburg again. I don't want to leave Smicksburg.*

As they made a turn into Macy's, she bumped into a tall man. He leaned over and Lexi read his sign: *Homeless. Need money.* He held up a brown paper bag.

Shame washed over Lexi. Her dad had begged for money like this, only to come home and laugh at all the suckers who donated to a so-called homeless man. "Get away from me," she yelled.

Elyse spun around, took her hand and faced the man. "What's wrong?"

He staggered. "Do you have a dollar?"

Elyse dug into her purse and pulled out a five dollar bill. "Here you go. Merry Christmas."

Ali shook his hand. "Yes, Merry Christmas."

She nudged Lexi, but she put her hands behind her back and glared at the man.

"Have a good day," Ali offered, linking her arm through Lexi's. Steering her toward Macy's, Ali blurted, "Why so rude?"

"He'll only buy beer."

"What?"

"He smelt like alcohol. He's a drunk."

They stopped again and Elyse gave Ali a knowing look. "I just gave a birthday gift to Jesus. Remember mom always says

Christmas is Jesus' birthday and we get party favors? It's about Him. Well, how do you give Jesus a present? By doing something for the least of these."

"Least of these?" Lexi asked. "He's a drunk and will only use that money for more beer."

"How do you know?" Ali asked. "And if he does, God loves him. Why all this fuss?"

"Alcohol," Lexi blurted. "God hates it. He hates how it makes people cruel!"

"Oh, honey," Elyse said. "Like your dad?"

Lexi stomped her foot. "Yes. God hates what it did to me."

Ali hugged her. "Yes, God does hate that, but He came for people who need help."

Lexi wanted to run. Run and scream. *She needed help when a little girl. No one was there for her.* Mr. Beech came to her mind and his dog that protected her. And then Mrs. Peters from across the street who also tried to help. Was God helping her back then? Was he helping now?

Tears steamed down her cheeks and Elyse and Ali pulled her into a nearby coffee shop. "Let it out, Lexi," Ali said.

They sat her down at a small round table and took both of her hands. "Lexi," Elyse said, rubbing her hand. "You're never going back to an abusive home. You know that, right?"

Lexi didn't know anything so she only shook her head.

"Judy's a good social worker and won't let that happen."

"Why all the secrets?" Lexi managed to say. "Something's changing."

Elyse tightened her grip. "Trust us. It's a good change."

"Yes," Ali said, "a very good change, but we can't tell you because…it takes time."

Lexi calmed down and her heart began to smile. *Of course. It takes time to be Amish.*

Chapter 13

Love Really Came Down At Christmas!

Lexi sat next to Emma at the Amish Christmas Eve program in the one-room schoolhouse. "Why isn't this on Christmas Eve if it's a Christmas Eve program?" she asked.

"Folks are traveling far to see loved ones. So, we're having it now."

"But it's not Christmas Eve…"

"We Amish celebrate Christmas on many days. Big families and so we need more than one day."

Lexi smiled. She was going to love being Amish. She even had a part to play in this program and she knew this was a clue to the whole secret. It was so obvious. It wasn't by chance that she'd be passing out heart ornaments the whole school made with Emma's help.

Ida opened the program by welcoming everyone and then in a clear voice sang:

Love came down at Christmas,
Love all lovely, Love Divine,

Love was born at Christmas,
Stars and Angels gave the sign.
Worship we the Godhead

Ida gasped and then ran off the platform without finishing the song. The sound of a woman weeping was heard from behind and Lexi turned to see Marie sobbing, clenched on to a teenaged boy. Ida kissed him on the cheek and hugged him.

Emma stood. "Matthew. My Matthew."

Lexi glared. This was the shunned grandson? The one who left, breaking Emma's heart? He didn't even come for Atley's funeral. But here he was, acting as if nothing happened and the Amish were kissing him. Men and women were both kissing him on the cheek.

Levi strode over to his son, squeezing his shoulder and leaning down as Matthew whispered in his ear. Levi embraced his son and kissed his cheek. He led him to the platform and through tear streaked cheeks said, "My son's come back. He sees the error of his ways. He'll be making a kneeling confession come Sunday.

"I'd kneel right here and say how sorry I am to you all," Matthew said eagerly. "The bishop and I have some talking to do first."

"Welcome back, Matthew," someone yelled.

Heads nodded in agreement.

"I don't deserve to be accepted back in, but I'll be doing my best to keep my vow, with God's help."

Lexi turned to Emma whose face was lit up like she'd just seen an angel, and fear arose in Lexi. If Matthew wasn't gone, she couldn't take his place. A pain shot through her stomach and she gasped.

Emma turned to her. "Lexi, you okay?"

"No," she cried. "Stomach ache. Can I leave?"

"I'll have someone drive you home."

"We walked and….White's tied outside. Angela won't mind."

Giving her a hug, Emma whispered in her ear, "You go on. I'll pass out the hearts."

Lexi pulled away and darted to the back of the schoolhouse and out the door.

~*~

Lexi wanted to stay in bed and not attend the town Light Up. Her hopes of being Ida's sister and Emma's granddaughter over the past two days were dashed to pieces. Matthew was the new hero in town, all anyone talked about. He didn't deserve all the worship lathered on him by Amish and non-Amish alike, but there he was, strutting around town, visiting people, asking for forgiveness while everyone applauded.

"Lexi, can I come in?" Ali asked. "Want to show you

something."

"Alright."

Ali flew open the door and twirled into the room. "How do I look?"

Lexi had to admit, she loved the boots, black sweater and new jeans. "Nice."

"How do I look?" Elyse asked, walking in, nose in the air. "I feel like a million bucks in this outfit."

New boots, jeans and the same style sweater as Ali's, only red.

"And how do I look?" Angela asked, face red. "I know, just like the girls, only in a green sweater."

Lexi gawked. "Angela, you look so…"

"Young," Elyse blurted. "Mom's too hard on herself. She looks great in her outfit."

Angela stared at Lexi with misty eyes.

John came into the room with a box wrapped with red and white striped paper and placed it on Lexi's bed. "For you."

Lexi studied Angela and John. They seemed happier than usual, but it was Light Up Night. John was probably excited to see the nativity set with live animals on display for all the town and tourist to see, especially his hero, Joseph. "Thank you." She ripped it open to find jeans, boots, and a white sweater that matched everyone else's. "Thanks," she said, a little confused. *Why all this matching stuff*, she wondered.

"We'll leave while you get dressed," Angela said.

"I am dressed. Wearing this."

"No, silly," Ali said, rubbing Lexi's head. "Put on your new outfit and meet us downstairs. It's important."

"Yes," Elyse said, clapping her hands. "Hurry up."

Lexi near jumped into her outfit after they left and her head spun. This was her second Christmas with the Stotlers, but nothing like this had ever happened. Why did they all have to wear the same things? She pulled the sweater over her head, ran to her dresser to smooth her hair, and made her way downstairs.

Sitting around the Christmas tree was the Stotler family, Angela leaning against John, tears running down her face.

"My last Christmas here, huh?"

"No," John said, "we're your Christmas present, if you want us."

Lexi thought the colored lights on the tree were more vivid.

"What do you mean?"

"The secret we've been keeping. It's over." Angela said, choking on tears. "We can adopt you."

"If you don't want to be Amish," Ali said, laughing.

Lexi blinked uncontrollably and felt frozen in time. "You want me?"

John nodded. "We worked on Joseph for a reason. I

wanted to explain how love came from God. Remember how I told you how God gave Joseph love for Jesus."

Lexi nodded.

"It's how we all feel about you. Can we be your family?"

Lexi's knees felt weak. Was she dreaming? John's eyes begged her to give an answer. She clearly saw love in his eyes.

"Please?" John asked again, arms open wide.

Lexi ran to him and squeezed his neck. "Thank you."

"Thank *you*," John said.

~*~

Lexi held a candle up to the twinkling stars above. She wasn't alone anymore but it would take a while to believe it all. No more moving around, but she would now be Lexi Stotler. She reached for Angela's hand as the tree lit up. As everyone cheered, Angela leaned down to kiss Lexi's cheek. "Your my girl now," she beamed.

Lexi could barely take it all in. She'd be staying in Smicksburg. This beautiful little town, now aglow in candlelight as hundreds of people met at the Christmas Tree at the entrance of Old Smicksburg Park.

Angela turned to the children's choir and held up a hand and they all started to sing:

Love came down at Christmas,
Love all lovely, Love Divine,
Love was born at Christmas,

Stars and Angels gave the sign.

Worship we the Godhead
Love incarnate, love divine
Worship we our Jesus
But wherewith for sacred sign?

Love shall be our token,
Small gift until something greater is given
Love shall be yours and love be mine,
Love to God and all men,
Love for plea and gift and sign.

Cheers went up and the crowd began to mingle. Angela led her across the street to the church. "Another surprise."

As the mounted the church steps, they crossed to where hot chocolate and cookies were being served. A man wearing a Santa hat bellowed, "Ho ho ho."

Lexi gasped. "Sam?"

He chuckled. "I'm Davy Crockett, don't you remember?"

"What are you doing here?"

"Well, young lady, first I need to thank you and White for saving my life. I fell and didn't know who or where I was. You brought help to me."

"It was White who did that. He heard your harmonica."

"Well, I'm grateful to you both. Got a job and a house,

too."

"Really? Where?" Lexi asked, happy to see Sam look so great.

"You're in it. I'm the new church janitor. Gus retired. I have a room upstairs, all snug and cozy. Pastor Dale said I have free run of the place, within reason," he winked. "He gave me a few rules, like don't go chasing people away by telling them to get off Indian Territory." He poured two mugs filled with hot chocolate and then made one for himself. "Lift up your glasses for a toast. I say thank God for little angels like Lexi. God bless her."

Lexi couldn't believe her ears. Was she like an angel to Sam the way Mr. Beech had been for her?

John tapped Lexi's shoulder. "Time for family pictures in front of the tree." He grinned. "Notice anything?"

Angela eyes glimmered. "Yes, John. I notice."

Lexi was so enthralled, she wouldn't notice anything different if it up and smacked her in the head. "No," she said.

John pulled down his V-neck sweater and pointed to his tie. "My tie has all the colors of my family. Will make a nice picture." He smirked. "Sorry. I saw the nerdy tie you got me on Black Friday. Wouldn't wear it."

Angela let out a howl. "Yes you would if I hadn't bought this plaid one."

Lexi stared at John's tie. It was red, white, black and

green, the colors of all the women's sweaters. A sense of belonging overwhelmed her and she hugged John around the middle. "Thank you. And you're not a nerd."

He embraced her and the feelings she so longed for, the love of a father, enveloped her. John kissed her head. "Love you, Lexi."

"Me, too," she was able to get out.

As they walked to get into line for a picture in front of the tree, Lexi spied Emma getting out of Elyse's car, White accompanying them. As they approached, Lexi ran to Emma. "Did you hear? I'm going to be adopted!"

Emma's face split into a toothy smile. "I told you to trust me that there'd be a big surprise for Christmas."

"So you knew all along?"

"*Jah*, I did," Emma said, taking Lexi's hand. "Paperwork had to be finalized and all, so I had to keep it under my bonnet," she quipped. "*Jah*. The Good Lord above heard my prayers. Matthew's back with a repentant heart and Lexi Remington has a home right next door. Praise be."

John gave Emma a side-hug. "Can't you be in the family picture? Just once?"

Emma guffawed. "*Nee*. You know Amish ways."

Lexi knew the Amish didn't believe in taking their picture, but she couldn't help but ask. "How about if you're turned side-ways, your big black bonnet covering your face. Please?"

Emma chuckled. "I won't be bending the rules. I'll stand here and watch as the Stotlers take a new family picture."

Ali and Elyse slipped into line and soon they were up, a photographer ready to take their picture. Lexi sat in between John and Angela, White at her feet, while Ali and Elyse stood in the back. Lexi felt nestled in love as she met Emma's gaze. Joy like she'd never experienced made her eyes moist. *Thank you, Lord*, she prayed. *You answered my biggest prayer.*

The photographer asked them to say 'Cheese', which they did and stepped off the little platform. A very unwelcome thought darted into Lexi's mind and she gasped. Emma noticed and held her by the shoulders. "Your stomachache's back?"

"I can't be adopted. What will I tell the kids at school? They think my parents are living in France!"

Ali and Elyse giggled, but John hushed them. "I guess we can't wait until Christmas morning for another surprise."

"Another surprise?" Lexi asked, feeling her legs turn to jelly. *Hope it's a good one.*

Angela clapped her hands rapidly as she near danced on her toes. "I'm going to homeschool you. You seem to learn better that way. Would you like that?"

Lexi leaned into Emma for support. "Can you get sick from being too happy? I feel dizzy."

Angela wagged a finger. "If you can get sick for being too

happy, don't use it as an excuse to get out of school, okay?"

Lexi embraced Angela. "Okay."

As she tried to relax in Angela's arms, Lexi tilted her head and looked at the stars. She noticed all the constellations John had tried to teach her. And for the first time, a lone star didn't seem isolated, but a part of a picture. *Thank you, Lord. This is the best Christmas ever. I think I know what love is and where it came from: a little baby in a manger, loved and adopted, just like me.*

Hot Chocolate Christmas Gift Instructions

In all my books I leave recipes at the end. There was a lot of hot chocolate over at Emma Yoder's, so here's a very simple and cost effective hot chocolate mix. I've given it as Christmas presents and it's always a hit. Put mix in a mason jar and wrap a ribbon around the top. Attach recipe to the ribbon by using a hole punch.

Homemade Hot Chocolate Mix

2 c. powdered milk

1 ¼ c white sugar

½ c unsweetened cocoa (bakers cocoa)

Amish Christmas Cookie Recipes

In my *Amish Knitting Circle: Smicksburg Tales 1*, I have many Amish Christmas cookie recipes that my friends in Smicksburg shared with me, and they are *very* good! I'd like to share them with you. Enjoy!

Lydia's Sugar Cookies with Cinnamon Frosting

3 c. Crisco

2 c. white sugar

2 c. brown sugar

5 eggs

3 c. whole milk

Vanilla to flavor (1 tsp.)

6 tsp. baking powder

3 tsp. baking soda

Pinch of salt

Enough flour to handle, not too much. About 9 cups.

Cream shortening with sugars. Add wet ingredients. Sift dry ingredients and slowly fold in. Mix well. Drop teaspoon full of batter on cookie sheet. Bake at 375 for 8-10 minutes.

Cinnamon Frosting

1 c. Crisco

3 c. powdered sugar

1 tsp. vanilla

Pinch salt

Milk to thin a bit

Flavor with cinnamon to your liking.

Ginger Cookie

1 c brown sugar

1 c. shortening (Crisco)

½ c. hot water

1 egg

2/3 molasses

1/3 c. corn syrup

1 T baking soda

1 T cinnamon

1 T Ginger

1 T vanilla

Pinch salt

1 T baking powder

Enough flour to make soft dough. Start with 4 cups to start. Add flour slowly until right consistency.

Sift flour with salt and spices. Cream shortening and sugar; add egg and beat until light. Add molasses, corn syrup and vanilla, then dry ingredients. Dissolve baking powder in hot water, and add to mix. Add flour, not to exceed 9 cups. Drop by teaspoons on greased cookie sheet. Bake for 10 minutes at 350 degrees.

Oatmeal Whoopie Pies

4 c. brown sugar

1 ½ c. Oleo (Crisco)

4 eggs

4 c. flour

4 c. oatmeal

2 t. cinnamon

2 t. baking powder

2 t. baking soda dissolved in 6 T boiling water

Cream together sugar, Oleo, and eggs. Add pinch of salt, flour, oatmeal, cinnamon, baking powder. Add soda water last.

Beat and drop by teaspoon full on greased cookie sheet. Bake at 350 degrees. Take two cookies and spread with filling, holding them together.

Whoopie Pie Filling

2 egg whites

2 t vanilla

4 T flour

4 T milk

4 c. powdered sugar

1 c. Crisco

Beat egg whites until stiff. Add other ingredients. Spread between cookies and enjoy.

Chocolate Whoopie Pies

4 c. flour

2 c. sugar

2 t. soda

1 ½ salt

1 c. shortening (Crisco)

1 c. cocoa

2 eggs

2 t vanilla

1 c. sour milk from the cow (or 1 tablespoon of lemon juice or vinegar plus enough milk to make 1 cup)

1 c. cold water

Cream: sugar, salt, shortening, vanilla and eggs. Sift: flour, soda and cocoa. Mix ingredients together and slowly add sour milk and water until right consistency. Can add flour to mixture if too gooey. Drop by teaspoonful. Bake at 350. Put two cookies together with Whoopie Pie Filling recipe.

Christmas Butter Cookies

3 c. powdered sugar

½ c. white sugar

2 c. butter

2 tsp. vanilla

3 eggs, beaten

6 c. flour

Cream together butter and sugars, add vanilla and eggs. Mix well and add flour and baking powder. Roll thin and cut. Bake at 350 degrees. Top with frosting.

Basic Cookie Frosting

3 egg whites

$\frac{1}{2}$ tsp. cream of tartar

4 c. powdered sugar

Water

Beat egg whites and cream of tartar. Add powdered sugar and beat until stiff. Add enough water so that you can dip the cookies in the frosting.

Butterscotch Cookies

2 cups brown sugar

3 eggs

1 cup shortening or lard

4 cups flour

1 tsp. baking soda

1 tsp. cream of tartar

1 cup nuts

Mix all ingredients except nuts. Stir the nuts in by hand. Roll the dough into tubes 2 inches thick and cut in thin slices. Press with fork or potato masher to make design. Bake at 350 for 8-12 minutes.

About the Song "Love Came Down At Christmas"

Love Came Down At Christmas was written by Christina Rossetti who was a Victorian poet (1830 1894). The simplicity of the song is to reflect the simplicity of the Christmas message. God incarnate came into the world to show His love. She based the song on the following scriptures, full of repletion concerning love: 1 John 4: 7-12

> *Dear friends, let us love one another, for love comes from God. Everyone who loves has been born of God and knows God. Whoever does not love does not know God, because God is love. This is how God showed his love among us: He sent his one and only Son into the world that we might live through him. This is love: not that we loved God, but that he loved us and sent his Son as an atoning sacrifice for our sins. Dear friends, since God so loved us, we also ought to love one another. No one has ever seen God; but if we love one another, God lives in us and his love is made complete in us.*

To hear this song sung on YouTube, click link below:

https://www.youtube.com/watch?v=gMcIA9ghNhg

Merry Christmas! I hope this little book will help you in some small way know the love of God in your own heart. Blessings! Karen Anna Vogel

About Author Karen Anna Vogel

Karen Anna Vogel has worn many hats: stay-at-home mom to four kids, (youngest daughter Kara Vogel Farnam is a buddy Amish fiction author), home school vet, entrepreneur (started Thrifty Christian Shopper) substitute teacher (aka survivor) wife to Tim for 33 years, musician. Writing has always been a constant passion, so Karen was thrilled to meet her literary agent, Joyce Hart, in a bookstore...gabbing about Amish fiction.

After her kids flew the coop, she delved into writing, and nine books later, she's passionate about portraying the Amish and small town life in a realistic way, many of her novels based on true stores. Living in rural, PA, she writes about all the beauty around her: rolling hills, farmland, the sound of buggy wheels.

She's a graduate from Seton Hill University (psych & education) and Andersonville Theological Seminary (Masters in Biblical Counseling). In her spare time she enjoys knitting, photography, homesteading, and sitting around bonfires with family and friends. Visit her at www.karenannavogel.com

Karen's works so far:

Continuing Serials:

Amish Knitting Circle: Smicksburg Tales 1

Amish Knitting Circle: Smicksburg Tales 2

Amish Knit Lit Circle: Smicksburg Tales 3

Amish Knit & Stitch Circle: Smicksburg Tales 4

Novels:

Knit Together: Amish Knitting Novel

The Amish Doll: Amish Knitting Novel

The Herbalist's Daughter Trilogy

Novellas:

Amish Knitting Circle Christmas: Granny & Jeb's Love Story

Amish Pen Pals: Rachael's Confession

Christmas Union: Quaker Abolitionist of Chester County, PA

How to Know the Love of God

God so loved the world, that He gave His only Son, that whoever believes in Him should not perish but have eternal life. *John 3:16*

God so loved the world

God loves you!

"I have loved you with an everlasting love." — Jeremiah 31:3

"Indeed the very hairs of your head are numbered." — Luke 12:7

That He gave His only Son

Who is God's son?

"Jesus answered, 'I am the way and the truth and the life. No one comes to the Father except through me.'" — John 14:6

That whoever believes in Him

Whosoever? Even me?

No matter what you've done, God will receive you into His family. He will change you, so come as you are.

"I am the Lord, the God of all mankind. Is anything too hard for me?"
— Jeremiah 32:27

"The Spirit of the Lord will come upon you in power, ... and you will be changed into a different person." — 1 Samuel 10:6

Should not perish but have eternal life

Can I have that "blessed hope" of spending eternity with God?

"I write these things to you who believe in the name of Son of God so that you may know that you have eternal life." - 1 John 5:13

To know Jesus, come as you are and humbly admit you're a sinner. A sinner is someone who has missed the target of God's perfect holiness. I think we all qualify to be sinners. Open the door of your heart and let Christ in. He'll cleanse you from all sins. He says he stands at the door of your heart and knocks. Let Him in. Talk to Jesus like a friend…because when you open the door of your heart, you have a friend eager to come inside.

Bless you!

If you have any questions, contact Karen at
www.karenannavogel.com

Made in United States
Orlando, FL
18 November 2022